MAVERICK MAKERS

**Center Point
Large Print**

**This Large Print Book carries the
Seal of Approval of N.A.V.H.**

MAVERICK MAKERS

DANE COOLIDGE

CENTER POINT PUBLISHING
THORNDIKE, MAINE

This Center Point Large Print edition
is published in the year 2005 by arrangement with
Golden West Literary Agency.

Copyright © 1931 by Dane Coolidge.
Copyright © renewed 1958 by Nancy Roberts Collins.

The text of this Large Print edition is unabridged. In other
aspects, this book may vary from the original edition. Printed in
Thailand. Set in 16-point Times New Roman type.

ISBN 1-58547-528-9

Library of Congress Cataloging-in-Publication Data

Coolidge, Dane, 1873-1940.
    Maverick makers / Dane Coolidge.--Center Point large print ed.
    p. cm.
    ISBN 1-58547-528-9 (lib. bdg. : alk. paper)
    1. Large type books. I. Title.

PS3505.O5697M388 2005
813'.52--dc22

2004014989

CONTENTS

CHAPTER I
A Great Mistake

IT WAS FREEZING cold when Number Nine, west-bound, rumbled down out of Puerco Pass and whistled to stop at Bitterwater. Cold with snow on the ground—and a sandstorm a thousand feet high, rolling in from the dry river-bed beyond. The air was full of grit and spitting with electricity and the sun hung blood-red in the west, but down at the station a hundred cowboys were waiting and when the engine stopped for water they cursed.

A bass drum boomed twice, someone emptied a six-shooter; and then on the rear platform a lone man appeared, leaning out to look ahead. All they could see was a big wolfskin overcoat, and the top of a brown derby hat.

"Is that him?" yelled a dozen eager voices at once; and a big man answered contemptuously,

"Hell, no! Can't you see that cady hat?"

But the man in the derby drew a pistol from his belt and slipped it into his overcoat pocket. He had expected something like this.

The train jerked forward and rumbled slowly down the track, to deliver its passengers at the station; and Jeff Standifer, still watching from the platform, was conscious of a woman beside him. A very pretty woman, gowned in the latest New York style, and when she beheld the huge crowd she shrank back.

"Oh, dear!" she cried, as another gun went off. And involuntarily she glanced at Standifer.

"Never mind," he said. "They won't hurt a lady. That bunch is waiting for me."

"No, they aren't!" she replied. "They're waiting for *me*. Did you ever make a great mistake?"

He glanced at her over his shoulder as he sized up the milling crowd.

"Lots and lots of 'em," he answered grimly. "But this last one is the worst of all. That's the Rustlers' Union, unless I'm badly mistaken, down to run me out of town."

"No, no," she insisted, laughing nervously. "They're good boys—I know every one of them. I used to live here at Bitterwater. And they've come down to welcome *me*. Only—oh, I'm in a terrible fix!"

She gazed at him appealingly, but he did not respond. She doubted if he had even heard.

"I—I don't know you," she went on, "nor what your mistake was. But mine was a thousand times worse."

"You're wrong," he said, drawing back. "That gang is out to kill me."

"Why, you're crazy!" she cried, almost in tears. "Can't you hear them shouting: 'Annabelle!' And oh, they've got a bull-fiddle!"

She clasped her hands in horror as a raucous roar went up and he looked the crowd over again, doubtfully.

"Well, maybe you're right," he admitted. "But there seem to be two different outfits. And I just got a telegram, on the train, warning me not to get off at Bitterwater. That being the case, and with a fight on my hands, I don't suppose I can be of much assistance to you. But—"

"Oh, yes, you can!" she exclaimed, suddenly clutching his arm as the train came to a grinding stop. "Just let me walk along with you until we get to the hotel and I'll never, never forget it!"

"Yours to command!" he responded gallantly. "Play your cards and I'll follow suit. Only just take my *left* arm, lady, in case—"

His words were lost in the sudden din of cow-horns and the jangle of a restaurant triangle. Resin-boxes brayed and trumpets blared, and above the boom of the big bass drum the bull-fiddle let out a roar. It was a frontier *charivari* and the porter dropped down grinning to place his upholstered step for the bride. But all this was lost on Standifer for, looming head and shoulders above the crowd, he saw a man with death in his eyes.

"That's Jack—Jack Flagg!" spoke a voice in his ear. And Jeff nodded, still watching his man.

"Don't be afraid," he said. "I'll protect you, whatever happens."

"But I *am* afraid!" she faltered, clutching convulsively at his arm. And as she spoke Flagg started towards them.

He was a tall man, nearly six feet six, with broad, menacing shoulders and spidery legs which came to a point in a pair of slim, high-heeled boots. He was a handsome man, too, but his face was flushed with drink and there was a dangerous glare in his eyes. It

9

was a look which Standifer had come to know and he dropped his right hand into his pocket.

The roar of the bull-fiddle had suddenly ceased, the drums and horns were stilled, and in the silence Jack Flagg spoke.

"Hello, Annabelle!" he greeted, barring their way. "Who's this?" And he pointed to Standifer.

For a moment she stood mute, her eyes searching desperately for some friendly face in the crowd. Then she glanced up at Jeff with a swift, radiant smile.

"Why—why, this is my husband, Jack."

Standifer started and for an instant his poker-face changed. Then, reading the fear in her dark appealing eyes, he drew down his lips and said nothing.

"The hell it is!" jeered Flagg, looking Jeff over insolently. "So you married this thing, eh? A New York dude, with a cady hat and everything! Well, come on, boys—let's kiss the bride!"

He reached out to snatch her, but before he could claim his kiss the girl slapped him, full in the face. All her fear had vanished now and she confronted him defiantly, unmindful of the man at her side. Flagg stepped back swiftly, his cheeks pale except for the brand where her hand had left its mark, and Standifer caught his eye.

"Kindly leave the lady alone," he suggested. And the cowboy turned on him furiously.

"You poor, damned yap," he cursed. "Who called you in on this? Annabelle is my girl and I'm going to have that kiss. We'll just see what you're going to *do* about it!"

He shot out a long arm and made a grab at Annabelle; and Jeff's hand whipped out of his overcoat. A heavy pistol flashed in the air and came down on Flagg's head and he fell like a pole-axed steer. Standifer looked at the crowd, his blue eyes turning steely grey, but his voice was still pitched low.

"Anyone else want a kiss?" he asked. And they opened up to let him pass.

CHAPTER II
The Newly-Weds

WITH THE BLUSHING bride on his arm and his six-shooter ready at hand, Jeff Standifer passed swiftly through the gawking crowd, which had divided once more into two groups. On the left, grim and hostile, stood men fresh from the range with their pistols hung rustler style. And on the right, grinning and sheepish, stood the cowboy musicians, their instruments still in their hands.

"Hello, Johnny!" cried Annabelle, who had suddenly regained her spirits. "I knew I'd find you here, somewhere. Say, George, will you bring my bags? We're going to Mother Collingwood's hotel."

She glanced up at Standifer as, his poker face still set, he scanned the ranks of the rustlers, and his white teeth flashed back a slow smile.

"This is a new one on me," he said. "But stay with it—I'm game. Who are these boys with the drums and horns?"

"Oh, some cowboys I know," she answered airily. "They're just out for a little fun."

"Yes, they seem to be right playful," responded Jeff. "Sorry I had to hit your friend, but his head felt good and hard, so I reckon there's no real harm done."

"Well—perhaps not," she sighed. "But I'm afraid he won't like it. You see, Jack and I were engaged."

"The hell!" exclaimed Standifer, startled out of his calm. "So that's what was biting him. But all the same, when a lady refuses a kiss—"

"Yes!" she prompted, meeting his eyes mischievously.

"Never mind," he said. "We'll discuss that later. Who is this Jack Flagg, anyhow?"

"Why, he's Father's range boss. The Mill Iron outfit, you know. And—"

"Holy smoke!" burst out Jeff, suddenly looking her over again. "Are you Captain Bayless' daughter?"

"Shhh!" she whispered fiercely. "You're supposed to know all that! Don't forget—we're newly-weds!"

"Well, tell me a little more, before I get in worse!" he entreated. But the bull-fiddle had set up its roar. The horns and drums joined in, then the gong and the resin-boxes; and as they started up the street a procession fell in behind, with the *charivari* band up in front.

"Let's hurry!" gasped Annabelle and, running hand-in-hand, they came once more to where a human voice could be heard.

"That's the Company Headquarters, down there," she explained as they paused for breath. "But we'll stop when we get to the hotel. Mother Collingwood will take me in and—well, you see Father married again and perhaps I wouldn't be welcome. Did you ever have a stepmother?"

"Stepfather—just as bad," he answered. "Is this the hotel, ahead?"

He pointed to a large and pretentious building, constructed of sandstone from the neighboring buttes, and Annabelle dimpled into laughter.

"That's the Bucket of Blood," she shouted into his ear. "The finest saloon in town. They had a fight there one time and two men were killed at once. And before the coroner came they had bled so much the boys named it the Bucket of Blood."

"Quite a burg!" he observed, surveying the single street with its long row of adobes and false fronts. "But who are these gentlemen that are following so close? I suppose they're some more of your friends?"

"Well, not all," she admitted after a hasty look behind. "That big man with the red beard is Hog-eye Bill Longyear. He calls himself the Rustler King."

Jeff glanced back again and leaned closer to her ear.

"I was called out here by your father," he confided, "to put the fear into these rustlers. And I believe they've caught on who I am."

She looked up at him, startled, then back at the gang of rustlers who were rushing up to cut them off.

"You're perfectly safe—with me," she said. "Don't forget now—you're Annabelle's husband."

"I'm sure glad to know it," he responded enigmatically as the mob closed in around him. And he stopped short, with his back to the wall.

Once more he stood facing them, one hand in his overcoat pocket, and the tumult and shouting ceased. The rustlers drew together, looking him over with hateful eyes, and Bill Longyear stepped to the front. He was a big, burly man, with flaming red hair and beard, and he thrust his head out fiercely.

"I see," he observed, "you're wearing a pair of boots, in spite of your danged cady hat. Air you that ba-ad Texas Ranger that Captain Bayless sent fur?"

"Why, no," protested Annabelle, as Jeff did not answer. "This is my husband—from New York!"

"Excuse *me*, Miss Bayless," responded Longyear with mock politeness. "I happen to *know* about this hombre, myself. And I jest want to inform him, we're a committee of citizens to tell him he's not wanted in this town. Dropping down off the train like a regular city tough and belting Jack Flagg over the head! By grab, boys, we ought to lynch him!"

"Well, why don't you do it?" suggested Standifer ironically as a murmur went through the crowd.

"Aw—you and your big six-shooter and your little dicer hat!" blustered Longyear, drawing closer. "You must think, by Joe, we're skeered of you!"

"Oh, no," answered Jeff, as Annabelle clutched his arm. "But don't you ever think, Mr. Longyear, that I'm afraid of *you*. Because right there you'd be making a mistake."

"Oh, I would, hey?" jeered Longyear. "Well, I'd like to ask one question. What fur, then, did you wear that hard hat?"

"I wore it," retorted Standifer, "because it matches

14

the color of my hair and makes damned fools like you ask questions. But if you don't like my style you know what you can do. Just knock that hat off and see where you light. Or any other gentleman," he added.

He looked them over scornfully, his lips curling in a truculent smile, and Annabelle shrank away. But no one stepped out to smash the cady hat and he turned his attentions to Longyear.

"You were asking," he continued, "if I was that Texas Ranger that was due here on Number Nine.

Well, I'm the man, all right, and if any of you don't like it—"

"Oh, please don't talk like that!" broke in Annabelle anxiously. "Do you want to start a fight!"

"Never mind, now," he said. "I can do my own talking. These men have followed after me, and if they're looking for trouble I'll certainly do my best to accommodate them. I'm a free-born American citizen from the sovereign State of Texas and I'll wear any hat I please."

He pushed the derby on tighter and cocked his head at the crowd; but as he was turning away triumphantly the doors of the Bucket of Blood bulged outward and a big, rawboned cowboy lurched forth. He was drunk, but not too drunk to take in the situation—the gang of menacing rustlers and the one man standing facing them, like a wolf before a pack of hounds. For a moment with drunken gravity he regarded Jeff Standifer and then with a loud whoop he surged over towards him, one hand raised high to strike.

"Hello, Good Eye, you danged old cow-thief!" he

yelped. And with a smashing blow he knocked the hat down over his ears, while the crowd as one man ducked. But the expected bullets did not come, and when they looked up Jeff was wrenching the hat from his ears, while a broad grin overspread his countenance.

"W'y, hel-lo, Rover!" he hailed. "I thought you were dead. Well, well, I'm sure glad to see you!" And he shot out a welcoming hand.

"Dead—nothing!" scoffed Rover, grabbing him into a bear-hug. "That bullet only creased me—made a nice part for my hair. Right there is where the old sheriff hit me." He backed off to show a white line through his bristling black hair, and then he looked at Jeff again. "But what the hell," he demanded, "are you doing with that thing on! Here, throw away that dicer and put on a man's hat!" He slammed his broad sombrero down on Jeff's rumpled hair and stood off to regard him admiringly.

"That's more like it!" he observed, casting the derby aside. "And boys," he went on, turning his grin on the crowd, "I want to introduce to you my old sidekick from New Mexico, the outstealingest danged cow thief in the world. This is Good Eye, boys, from the Seven Rivers country, where the kids cut their teeth on a running-iron. He can spot a slick-eared calf further than you yaps can see its dust. That's where he got his name, boys—Good Eye!"

He ended up with a resounding slap which made Standifer's head snap back, and threw out his chest dramatically.

"Hah—Good Eye!" he mocked. "The Maverick King. Twirling his twine he crouched behind a blade of grass, shouting: 'Whoopee-lah! *Orehanos!*' "

He went through the drunken motions of roping a calf as he let out the rustler war-cry, and Standifer shoved him rudely aside.

"That's a plenty now, Rover," he grinned. "I've been sent for, you might say, to discourage that kind of doings. And if you keep on talking these gentlemen might get the idea—"

"What!" yelled Rover. "Are you that cattle detective that the Old Man sent back to Texas for? Well, damn my heart, if that ain't the holy limit! Come on, this calls for the drinks!"

"Just a minute," broke in Standifer, as Rover laid hold of him. "I want to introduce you to the lady. Annabelle," he went on, "this is an old, old friend of mine. And Rover, shake hands with my wife."

"Your—wife!" quavered Rover. "My Gawd, are you married, too? Well, Jeff, you're sure getting respectable. Mrs. Standifer, ma'am, I want to congratulate you on getting a good husband like Jeff. He's a man you can depend on. He's never been known to weaken, and he's never hollered for help. That's his motto: 'Never holler for help.' "

"He never has—since I've known him," responded Annabelle demurely. "But don't you get my husband drunk, now!"

"No, ma'am," promised Rover, bowing low and crossing his heart. "Jest one drink, for old-time's sake. I'll bring him back as good as new."

"We'd better take her down to the hotel first," suggested Jeff. "I want to have a talk with you, Rover."

"Sure! Sure!" agreed Rover, brushing the staring rustlers aside as he escorted them to the door of the hotel; and the crowd looked on in wonder. Not in many a moon had things happened so thick and fast and still there was more to come.

The Hotel Bitterwater stood next to the Bucket of Blood—with another saloon on the other side—a two-storied stone building with a broad gallery above and below, in the old-fashioned Southern style. But that it was strictly respectable was evident at a glance, when Mother Collingwood came to greet them. She was a large and comfortable soul, with gray hair and a beaming smile, and when Annabelle ran to meet her she kissed her.

"Why, Annabelle!" she cried. "Is it true, what they say—that you're come back to Bitterwater, *married?*"

"I guess it is," admitted Annabelle, after returning the hearty kiss. "This is my husband, Mr.— er, Standifer. Can you give me a room for the night?"

She blushed rosy red as she took Jeff's arm and presented him to the keen-eyed hostess, and he concealed his embarrassment with a bow.

"Why, yes, child," responded Mrs. Collingwood, after a brief glance at Standifer and another and longer look at Rover, "you know you're always welcome. But I naturally thought, Annabelle, you'd go up to your father's and—"

"Oh, *you* know why I don't!" exclaimed Annabelle

impulsively. "I don't believe I'd be welcome. And your upstairs rooms are so nice and homelike—"

"I'll give you my best one, with the French doors on the gallery—"

"That will be just fine," dimpled Annabelle. "And now, Jeff, will you please register?"

"Oh—sure!" responded Standifer. And, stepping quickly to the front he wrote without a tremor:

"Jeff Standifer and wife, New York."

"What? From New York?" repeated Mother Collingwood. And she turned to eye Jeff suspiciously. "Yes, ma'am, New York," spoke up Rover with drunken confidence. "I *know* that's where he's from, because he had on one of them hard hats that they wear to protect their haids from the icicles. That's *my* hat he's got on now—I knowed him, back in New Mexico."

"Oh, I see," murmured Mrs. Collingwood; and Jeff broke the awkward silence by turning abruptly to Annabelle.

"I'm going to be busy," he said, "with some business for your father that may take me out of town. Will you be all right here with Mrs. Collingwood?"

"Why, bless her heart, yes!" cried Mother Collingwood. "I'll take the best of care of her, Mr. Standifer. But don't you go to drinking!" she charged; and gazed at Rover reproachfully.

"No, no!" laughed Jeff. "Just one glass with my old friend, here. But—er—Annabelle!" he went on, beckoning her over to one side.

"Yes—Jeff," she responded meekly.

"How are you fixed for money?" he asked, pulling out his roll.

"Oh, I've got plenty," she protested; but he peeled off three large bills and handed them over, negligently.

"Better take a little more," he observed. "In case I don't show up."

"Oh, thank you—Jeff," she murmured; and as she met his eyes she blushed again, rosy red. Then, chatting gaily with Mother Collingwood, she went up the winding stairs and Standifer hurried out with Rover. He felt the need of that drink.

CHAPTER III
The Captain

THERE WAS A WILD look in Standifer's eyes as he butted into the Bucket of Blood; and several rustlers at the bar, who had been denouncing him as a coward, stood frozen in their tracks. But the Ranger ignored them and signaled the bar-keeper.

"Gimme a tall one!" he said. And Rover smiled.

"That's the talk!" he applauded. "Give me a tall one, too."

But after the drink he plucked Jeff by the sleeve and beckoned him to a card-room in the rear.

"Now, what the hell," he demanded, "is all this about? And where did you meet up with Annabelle? She just came back from New York."

"I've been in New York, myself," defended Standifer. "Where do you reckon I got that hard hat?"

"Well, not in these parts," admitted Rover, sinking down and pushing the button for the drinks. "Do you figger that helped you to win her?"

"Didn't need no help!" answered Jeff. "And you don't need a drink, either. Keep sober—I want to talk to you."

"Because if you do," went on Rover. "I'm going to git me one. That's the finest gal in all this country. How'd you come to marry her, Jeff?"

"Say, you keep on asking questions and you'll know more than I do about this! So don't get so dadburned personal. What the devil are *you* doing, out in this part of Arizona? You don't mean to say you're on the dodge!"

"Yes, and don't *you* get too personal!" warned Rover jovially. "I'm Ralph the Rover—named after a dog—and I'm roving. Understand?

" 'Then Ralph the Rover tore his hair
And cursed himself in his despair.
But the waves rolled in on every side,
And the good ship sank beneath the tide.'

"I found that one time in a book of poetry—it's something about a pirate ship. Come on—let's have a drink!"

"One's all I need," responded Jeff shortly. "What I'm shy on is information, so taper off and tell me what you know."

"Yours truly," bowed Rover, after tossing off his whisky. "And Jeff, old-timer, if you need any assistance, jest call on me. Understand? I'll stay with you, fanning or fogging, until hell freezes solid. I never go back on a friend."

"I'm counting on you," answered Standifer. "You're the only friend I've got in the country, and I'm sure glad I ran across you. Now, who's this Jack Flagg, Rover?"

"Why, he's the lucky guy that was due to marry Annabelle. He's Captain Bayless' right hand man, and range boss for the Mill Irons. Didn't Annabelle tell you about him?"

"Not a word," stated Jeff, "until we stepped off the train and he tried to kiss the bride. I hit him over the head with my six-shooter."

"Well, say, you're getting bravo!" burst out Rover admiringly. "And I could see that Annabelle was pleased. Don't you remember what she said, when I mentioned that you'd never hollered for help? She knows now that she's married a real man!"

"Reckon so?" inquired Jeff. "But say, tell me this, then. Where do I get off with Captain Bayless? What's he going to say when I report at his office that I've just busted his range boss over the head?"

"You'd better not report it," advised Rover. "Because he thinks the world and all of Jack. Been his wagon-boss for years—and when he quit, last spring, the whole outfit went to hell. Drunk, tough and disorderly, and wouldn't work for old John Dobbins. So the Captain has jest hired back Jack."

"Well, I'm dished, then," sighed Jeff. "Unless," he added hopelessly, "I can make some grand-stand play and ketch one or two of these cow-thieves."

"You want a cow-thief?" barked Rover. "Want to ketch one, red-handed, before the old man hears from Jack? I can lead you right to the spot—I cut a blood-sign, coming to town!"

"You do it, offered Standifer, jumping up, "and I'll make you my side-kick on this job. I've got to have a pardner, and you're the very man I want, if you'll lay off of this sheepherder whisky."

"All right," agreed Rover. "Only I've got to have my dram or my mind don't seem to sagaciate. Let's go up to the Company House and see how Captain Bayless is taking it. If he's ca'm, he hasn't heard yet."

They slipped out the back way and passed up an alley, but as they came out on the street Jeff stopped.

"We'll have to get deputized first," he said. "Do you happen to know the sheriff?"

"Hell, yes," laughed Rover. "He just turned me out of jail last week. Best-hearted old sheriff you ever saw—can't bear to keep us boys locked up. Him and the J. P., they turn everybody loose."

"Well, that's fine," grumbled Standifer. "For getting votes, anyway. Reckon he'll turn all my rustlers loose, too?"

"You ain't caught any, yet," observed Rover with a grin. "There's the Headquarters Building, right ahead."

He pointed to a huge, two-story building that stood at the end of the street, and reluctantly Jeff walked down towards it. It too was made of sandstone, quarried out of the flat-topped buttes; and across the wide sidewalk, like an invitation to enter, there stretched a broad stream of light.

"That's his office," whispered Rover mysteriously, as they halted outside the door. "The old Cap'n is waiting—and he's shore on the prod," he added. "I'll bet you he's heard about Jack!"

He pointed in through the broad window and, pacing to and fro, Jeff caught the first glimpse of his employer. He was a stern-looking old man with a long moustache and a fierce goatee, and he stood up very straight, like a soldier. In his youth, as Standifer knew, he had been a Captain of Texas Rangers, when the Comanches were raiding the settlements. But now his hair and beard were snow-white, and his head was bowed in thought.

"I'll take a chance," decided Jeff. "All he can do is fire me. So you go down to the store and buy me a new hat. I'll meet you here in half an hour."

"Half a minute," corrected Rover, "if he knows you busted Jack. I don't care if you did marry Annabelle."

"Say, shut up about that," warned Standifer. "And get out of here, quick. He's coming!"

"Good evening," he greeted as the wide portal swung open; and Captain Bayless regarded him suspiciously.

"Good evening, sir," he answered, "and what is your business here? Didn't I hear another voice?"

He gazed into the darkness behind him, and Standifer broke into a sweat.

"I'm that Texas Ranger," he said, "that you wrote

Captain Ross for." And the old man regarded him sharply.

"Come in," he said at last; and when the door was closed he swung the heavy shutters across the window. "Now what's this I hear, about a fight at the station? Are you the man that got off that train?"

"Yes, sir," replied Standifer and Bayless glared at him angrily.

"I wired you," he said, "that the rustlers were gathering to run you out of town. Why didn't you go through, as I suggested, and leave the train at Duncan?"

"That isn't the way I work," responded Jeff. "I've come here to get my orders."

"Well, your orders," bellowed the Captain, "are to break up this damned thieving if you have to kill every rustler in the country. The Company is losing a thousand calves a year, to say nothing of the steers that are stolen. It has come to such a pass that every settler for a hundred miles thinks the Mill Irons ought to keep him in beef."

"That's the way it generally is," observed Jeff, philosophically, "where there's one big Company in the country. How's the sheriff—can you get him to deputize me?"

"Oh, yes, he'll do anything," answered Bayless savagely. "He's all things to all people—a great vote-getter and all that—but damn it, he never leaves town! You'll always find Smith Crowder down there on the saloon corner, or over playing pitch with his prisoners. They all like him, the old rascal, and I like him, myself. But what about my company and my obligation to the stockholders, who haven't received a dollar in years? I told Smith Crowder plainly I was out of patience with his tomfoolery and then I wrote John Ross for you. Sit down—have a drink! I forgot your name."

"Jeff Standifer," replied Jeff; and as Bayless went for the liquor he heaved a great sigh and sat down. The Captain had not heard about Jack Flagg being clubbed or he certainly would have mentioned it. Nor had he received the news of Annabelle's return, with Jeff tagging along as her husband. Otherwise there would have been some remarks, for the boss was not a man to mince words. But now he had his mind on the rustlers.

"There are three classes of people who are getting our cattle," began Bayless as he tossed off his drink. "The Mormons, back in the mountains and down along the river. My range boss is always having trouble with them. Then the Mexicans, over east and along the New Mexico line, are getting a world of beef. But my big trouble," and he frowned, "is with this gang of brazen rustlers who met you at the train tonight. I'll admit at the start that in any new country there's bound to be a certain amount of stealing. But when the rustlers get so bold that they try to run the country and dictate how I shall run my business, then it's time for the company to take the law in its own hands and fight the devil with fire. I want you, Mr. Standifer, to put the fear into their black hearts—and I'll stand by you, no matter who you kill."

He paused and nodded grimly, but Standifer only stirred in his chair.

"Well, as to killing," he said, at last, "that isn't the way I work. The theft of a few calves, or the beefing of a steer, would hardly justify that. I try to work within the law, but if a man resists arrest—"

"Ah, yes, yes!" beamed the Captain, pouring out another drink. "I quite understand you, Mr. Standifer. Just use your own judgment and you can always depend on me to come to your defense."

"Well—thanks," nodded Jeff. "I may have to call on you. But ordinarily I don't have any trouble. I try to work entirely through arrests and convictions. Can you depend on your district attorney?"

"As far," observed Bayless, "as any elective officer can be depended upon to prosecute his constituents. But the quick and easy way, as we found out back in Texas when the country was overrun with outlaws—"

"Nope," vetoed Standifer. "I'm no killer, Captain Bayless. I believe in respecting the law, and expecting others to do the same. That's the way to stamp out rustling."

"Oh, it is, eh?" blared the Captain, throwing back his mane of hair and glaring at Jeff ferociously. "Well, let's come to an understanding young man. Are you working for me, or am I working for you? That's what I want to know!"

"Well, neither one," responded Jeff. "I haven't taken the job yet. But if I do, Captain Bayless—"

"You'll tell me how to run things!" ended Bayless.

"No, by grab!" decided Standifer, rising up. "You

27

can get another man to do your killing."

"Oh, oh! Just a moment!" protested the Captain. "Now don't misunderstand me. You're a brave man, Mr. Standifer, or you'd have gone on to Duncan, instead of facing that crowd at the station. My old servant came running back and reported you'd had a fight, but he was so taken aback to see my daughter step down off the train that he couldn't give any details. It seems," he went on, falling to pacing the floor again, "that Annabelle is married."

"So I hear," responded Standifer bluffly.

"I've been expecting her," said Bayless, glancing uneasily towards the door. "But for some reason she hasn't come. I left the shutters open, to let the light pour out and indicate that she and her husband were welcome. But she must ask my forgiveness, and the forgiveness of her mother. There's someone out there, now!"

He hurried to the door and threw it open expectantly; but there in the bright light stood Ralph the Rover, his eyes squinted to a drunken leer.

CHAPTER IV
The Shivaree

THERE WAS MURDER in the old Captain's eyes as he glared into the face of Rover; and yet, before he spoke, he glanced behind him, out into the wind-swept night. But his daughter was not there and his rage burst forth like a torrent.

"What do you mean, you drunken fool?" he roared. "Begone! Get away from my door! No, I don't want to talk with you! Go!"

"Go, he says," observed Rover, winking solemnly at his friend behind; and Standifer saw a way out.

"Wait, Rover!" he called, "and I'll go along with you." But the Captain barred the door.

"Is this man," he demanded, "a friend of yours?"

"He sure is," responded Jeff, "and a damned good friend. We'll both of us go—right now."

He started to slip out the doorway but Captain Bayless stopped him, and suddenly his anger was forgotten.

"Well, I must say," he began, "you've got a strange taste in friends. This man was discharged by my range boss last week—something to do with stealing a calf—but of course, it's all right with me. What I wanted to say, before you go, was: You go ahead on that job and handle it to suit yourself. All I want, Mr. Standifer, is results."

He stepped aside to let Jeff pass, and his face took on a placating smile.

"You must excuse me," he murmured, "I'm not quite myself, tonight. I was expecting to find—Annabelle."

"Oh, she's gone to the hotel," spoke up Rover, unabashed. "And another thing, Captain. I wasn't fired—I quit. I've got too much brains to range-brand for the company for forty dollars a month. When I start to stealing, I'll steal for myself. Come on, Jeff, here's your hat."

He held up a brand-new, cream-colored Stetson, the best that money could buy, and Standifer slipped out the door.

"I don't know what you refer to," shouted Bayless over his shoulder; but Rover cut him short.

"I refer," he bawled back, "to Mr. Jack Flagg, and the calf he wanted me to steal. But I showed him, by grab, here's one cowboy he cain't intimidate. He's nothing but a widow-robbing crook."

Rover threw out his chest and surveyed the Captain arrogantly as he and Standifer traded hats, but Bayless waved him angrily away.

"Mr. Flagg informs me," he retorted, "that *you* are the crook. And between your word and his, I'll take Jack's."

"Help yourself!" returned Rover. "But what about this job, Jeff? Are we going out to ketch them rustlers?"

"What's that—what's that?" demanded the Captain breathlessly. And Jeff turned back to explain. "Well, by the gods!" moaned Bayless. "Must I take water again? Is this the man that informed you? Never mind my hasty words then. If they're butchering my steers you go ahead, Mr. Standifer, and arrest them."

"Well, what about Rover?" inquired Jeff, after a pause. "Do you reckon the sheriff will deputize him?"

"He'll have to do it," threatened the Captain, "or I'll cut off his tobacco money. I've been keeping him in cigars for years. But I don't give a damn who it is that arrests these cow-thieves as long as they're thrown into jail. It's been fourteen years by actual count since a rustler has been convicted in this county; but if that is your system, go ahead and play it out. And if the rascals resist arrest—"

"We'll kill 'em," croaked Rover. And once more Bayless' smile came back.

"I'll attend to this, right now," he announced, slamming the door; and as they stumbled across the tracks to where the jail and courthouse stood, Rover nudged Jeff in the ribs and laughed, slyly.

The sheriff's office and jail stood just behind the courthouse, connected by a bridge of sighs where the prisoners were led back and forth, and a strip of cement sidewalk below. A dim light within threw barred shadows across the windows, but as they tramped in the door they found the sheriff and three prisoners, engaged in a friendly game of pitch.

"Well, back to your cells, boys," he ordered, rising up; and Captain Bayless surveyed him scornfully.

"Smith," he said, "you haven't got the first idea of making this jail a place of punishment. Have a smoke," and he handed over a cigar.

The sheriff took it doubtfully, his keen eyes on Ralph the Rover who was standing defiantly in the rear.

"You, Rover!" he challenged, stepping towards him, "what the devil are you doing heah? I thought I told you to git out of town!"

"Important business," explained Rover, "made it necessary to return." And he jerked his head towards Bayless.

"Mr. Sheriff," began the Captain, "I'll make you

acquainted with Jeff Standifer, of the Texas Rangers. He's the man that Captain Ross sent out from San Antonio to help put a stop to this rustling."

"Delighted to know you, suh!" exclaimed the sheriff pompously as he extended a large, fat hand. "I've often heard Captain Bayless boast about the Texas Rangers, but you're the first one I ever saw."

He was a big man, rotund and smiling, with his trigger finger gone and a limp in one leg, which was short. But there was something about his smile and his round florid cheeks which made him look like an overgrown boy. Jeff shook hands, but he did not like him.

"Now, Smith," went on Captain Bayless, "I want everything to be regular. So please give Mr. Standifer a commission as deputy sheriff, and a star that he can wear around town. That will show he is authorized to make arrests."

For a moment the keen gray eyes of the sheriff squinted down as he glanced from man to man. Then he jerked open a drawer and brought out a star, which he pinned on Standifer's coat.

"I'll just deputize you, right now," he said, "and we'll talk about commissions later."

"All right," spoke up Rover, "you can give me one, too, Sheriff. We're going out to make an arrest."

"The hell you are!" bayed the sheriff. But when Bayless explained to him he dug up a star, reluctantly.

"That's all right, Captain," he protested, "but I've got my future to consider. And if it gits around the county that I've deputized this jail-bird I'm liable to hear from the voters. In jail one week and a deputy sheriff the next, don't look very regular, nohow. But if you'll vouch for him, Captain Bayless, and stand by if there's any trouble—"

"Give him the star," directed Bayless, "and I'll stand right behind you, no matter if all hell breaks loose. It has got to a point where I've got to stop this stealing or go out of business into bankruptcy."

"All right," grumbled Crowder as he pinned on the badge. "But remember now, Rover, the first time you git drunk—"

"Then down comes my meat-house," jested Rover.

"You're fired!" ended the sheriff, "and you'll serve out that sentence. Six months in the county jail."

"I'll remember," promised Rover; but as he passed out the door he polished up his badge with his sleeve.

"Put that under your coat," ordered Jeff severely, "and don't let me ketch you flashing it. Do you reckon the Texas Rangers go swelling around like that? Keep it hid. Well, good night, Captain!"

He shook hands perfunctorily with the General Manager of the Mill Irons and hired a horse at the O.K. Corral. But as he was saddling up, to get out of town, Rover stepped over and whispered in his ear.

"You ride down that street," he warned, "and these rustlers will follow you, savvy? Stick around a while until they git good and drunk—unless you want to take on the whole gang."

"Well, all right," spoke up Jeff. "We'll wait until tomorrow." And as he went out the gate he caught the roustabout grinning.

"Back to the Bucket of Blood," gloated Rover, "and we'll join hands in a regular bender. These rustlers have got spies, and that hostler is one of them; but getting drunk will throw them off their guard."

"If I wanted to get drunk," observed Jeff sarcastically, "I'd give five dollars for your start, right now. But maybe we'd better hide out. There's a lot of toughs in town, if I'm any judge, and these rustlers are sure on the prod."

"Out for trouble," agreed Rover as they dodged up the alley. "But they haven't forgotten Jack Flagg. They know from what you gave him you're not a man to be monkeyed with. And they know me, too—the scoundrels. It was only last week I took a crack at Jack, myself—that's how come they gave me six months."

"Oho!" laughed Standifer. "So that's what they were sore about."

"Yes, and that ain't all," returned Rover, rolling his eyes. "I know too much. Understand? I've got the goods on a lot of them. But they cain't touch me now—I'm a deputy sheriff!" And he slapped the star, under his coat.

"Yes, sir," he went on as they slipped into the card room and ordered a bottle brought in. "I'm a bad man from Bitter Crick, once I get my dander up; and this has made me hot as a fox. I'm going to take you, Jeff, to where a fresh beef has just been killed—there's blood-marks all over the ground. And leading off up the canyon is the tracks of their wagon-wheels, where they've gone on to make up a load. That's the way these rustlers work it—they kill and butcher a whole wagon-load. And if you run up on 'em, they shoot."

His deep-set eyes gleamed fiercely as he spoke, and he slapped his holstered six-shooter.

"But I'll show 'em," he boasted, "they cain't intimidate me! I'm a fighter! You know it—don't you?"

"I sure do," nodded Jeff. "What you been doing since I saw you last, that time when the sheriff shot you? I thought for a certainty, you were dead."

"Dead, hell," laughed Rover. "I jest let 'em think so, so the suckers would leave me alone. Been out here ever since, riding the range, and so forth, and I know this whole country like a book. W'y, Jeff, I can take you into some of the dangest places, where an officer never would go. And when it comes to rustling, I know the business from A to Z. Been in it, in fact, myself."

"I thought you might've," nodded Standifer, "but you don't need to tell *me* about it. And you don't need to tell on your friends. If I can't find 'em, they're welcome, that's all. I've had quite a little experience, back in Texas."

"Yes, but what's this you were telling me," spoke up Rover with wakened interest, "about being back in New York? By grab, when I saw you with that cady hat on—"

"Oh, that was just a bluff," laughed Jeff.

"What? Ain't you never been back there at all? Then what's all this about Annabelle?"

"I mean about the hat," hedged Standifer. "I just wore it to get into town."

"Yes, but listen," persisted Rover. "If you never went to New York—"

"Now, say, *you* listen," broke in Jeff, "and don't be so damned curious about something that's none of your business. I'm not prying into your past and don't you pry into mine. Is that agreeable? Then have a drink."

He poured out two glasses and as Rover tossed off his whisky he fell into a mellow philosophizing. He harked back to their early life, on the plains along the Pecos and catching cattle in the brakes of the Guadalupes; but in the midst of a rambling story he was brought to a halt by a noise like the roar of a bull.

"What's that?" he demanded, opening his mouth to listen. "By grab, it's the bull-fiddle! Them rascals have come back. Git for home, boy—this is your shivaree!"

Standifer listened, aghast, and from the street outside he could hear the *charivari* band tuning up. First the triangle, then the cow-horns, then the trumpets and drum—and last of all the great bull-fiddle with its resined, rawhide ropes, stretched taut across a box.

"My Lord!" he exclaimed, "I've got to get out of this!" But Rover cut him off at the door.

"None of that, now!" he warned. "Don't you skip out on Annabelle. Don't you leave her to face this alone. They'll keep it up all night unless you come out and make a speech, and invite them all in for the drinks."

"You buy 'em the drinks," implored Standifer desperately, slipping a couple of big bills into his hand.

36

"But so help me, Rover, this is asking too much. And some of these rustlers are liable to shoot me."

"Not with Annabelle there," answered Rover. "The boys would skin 'em alive. But I'll tell you right now, you've married the finest gal in all this country, and you've got to show a proper respect."

He took Standifer by one arm with such a compelling grip that resistance for the moment was useless. Jeff followed along reluctantly, out the door and up the alley, which Rover seemed to know like a cat; until at last, entering a back door, they found themselves in the Hotel Bitterwater, with Mother Collingwood running about like mad.

"Oh, Mr. Standifer," she implored, "please go up to the gallery before those drunken fools start to shooting. Because the last time they did this they broke six of my big windows and shot holes in my new, tin roof."

"Up he goes!" announced Rover, giving Jeff a final shove; and before he knew it he was pushed out on the upper gallery, full in the face of the yelling crowd. The bass drum boomed, resin-boxes and the bull-fiddle sent up a welcoming roar; but as Rover stepped forward and held up his hand the expectant cowboys fell silent.

"Gents and friends," began Rover, clearing his throat importantly as he took a fresh grip on Jeff, "it gives me great pleasure to introduce the bridegroom, who will speak a few words to you all."

Standifer glanced about helplessly, seeking some means of escape from the misguided officiousness of his friend. But Rover was inexorable and, on the brink of the abyss, he took the final step. If he could have escaped out of town before the *charivari* began, his brief pose as Annabelle's protector would be overlooked. But to appear outside her room, to make a speech as her husband—that was something that could never be condoned. He struck Rover fiercely away and when he addressed the crowd it was as Standifer, the cattle detective.

"I thank you, gentlemen," he began, "for the honor you have bestowed on me, but I'm afraid I don't deserve it. A man in my line of work can't expect to be real popular, so—"

"Bring out Annabelle!" shouted a voice and as if at a signal an inferno of noise broke loose. Jeff stepped back dizzily, his ordeal quickly over; but as he turned to beat a retreat he found Annabelle beside him, very charming in a smart negligee. For a moment their eyes met and at the appeal in her glance he forgot his craven intent. Bowing low he offered his arm and led her out on the gallery, where her appearance started a rousing cheer. Then as she gazed down at them, smiling, the macabre figures in the torchlight became still and attentive to her words.

"Thank you, boys," she said, "for this royal welcome home, even though it is a little noisy. I'm glad to be back in the old town again and to see so many of my friends. But my husband is kind of bashful on an occasion like this; so you'll all excuse him, I know."

She bowed and waved her hand and as they retired out of the glare Ralph the Rover leapt to the front.

"And now, gentlemen," he shouted in his big, rousing voice, "as a friend of the bride and groom, whom we all delight to honor, let me announce that the drinks are on me. So I ask you, one and all, to join me at the Bucket of Blood, where we will drink to their long life and happiness!"

He waved his hat and disappeared, leaping down the long stairs with the agility of a monkey; and from the darkness outside the drums and bull-fiddle gave a salute, before they were silenced in the rush for the bar.

Upstairs on the broad gallery, where but a minute before their ears had been assaulted by noise, Jeff and Annabelle stood alone—half stunned by the uproar, hardly knowing yet what they had done. They had acted upon impulse, in a desperate endeavor to cover up their first escapade. But now they were committed—to what?"

For a moment they stood staring, and Jeff wiped away the sweat as he faced the startled bride. Then he smiled and bowed gallantly, turning swiftly towards the stairs.

"Good night," he said. "I won't be coming back." And he hurried out into the dark.

CHAPTER V
Good Eye—The Texas Ranger

THERE WERE DRINKS, and more drinks, in the Bucket of Blood, and drunken men reeling down the street; but the man to whose health they drank—to his long life and happiness—was hiding in the alley behind. Things had happened too thick and fast for even Jeff Standifer, who prided himself on his nerve. He had been seized upon by circumstances and made the whim of hostile forces, until now he was hopelessly involved. In one night, in one hour, he had become so entangled that his only escape lay in flight. But he had put his hand to the plow.

He had come on from San Antonio as a representative of the Rangers, whose pride it was never to turn back; and if he took the train East without striking a blow he would cast dishonor on the force. Yet if he stayed, what explanations there were to be made! Was he married, or was he not? And had he a right to strike Jack Flagg over the head and leave him in a welter of blood? There would be hell to pay if the range boss learned the truth—and hell with the Captain, to boot—but Standifer had set out to run down Rover's rustlers and he hid in the alley and waited.

Men stumbled in and out of the Bucket of Blood or glided silently by. There was more on in the town than mere shouting and drinking, for the rustlers were still on his trail; but Jeff lurked in the shadows until Rover came out, muttering gloomily as he headed up the alley. They were alone, and Standifer followed boldly along behind him until, cursing, Rover whirled and drew his gun.

"Never mind, now, you danged drunken lout," spoke up Jeff. "Have you forgotten about those rustlers?"

"W'y, damn my heart," exclaimed the crestfallen Rover, "have you been waiting out here all night? I thought you was *married*, Jeff!"

"Let me do the thinking," grumbled Standifer, "and let's get out of town. I'll carry that whisky for you, too."

He snatched a quart bottle out of Rover's overcoat pocket and providently stowed it in his own. Then, down the echoing street, along the sidewalks of heavy planks, they made their way to the O.K. Corral; until at last, dim and muffled, they rode out of town and crossed the frozen river at the ford. The night was bitter cold, but the wind had gone down and the swoop of the sandstorm had ceased. Rover fell into a trail and headed south across the flats without a single word, and they settled in their saddles to endure.

Day dawned, a bleak gray, and the west wind came up again, whipping the sand up in gusts from the sand-washes; and as Jeff looked out over the bare and deserted country he shifted in his saddle and muttered. What malign fate had laid hold of him, after coming so far, and where would his misadventures end? Must he drift on endlessly behind his drunken guide, until they starved or froze in the snow?

Rover had huddled down inside his worn overcoat,

as uncommunicative as the sullen Comanches with whom his boyhood had been spent. The drink was dead in him now and he was back-tracking his own trail, where he had come down out of the hills. He was sober, but morose, and his flights of drunken oratory had been succeeded by a stoical calm. But he was awake and somberly vigilant, and as he rode his eyes searched the trail.

They toiled up a long rise to the summit of a ridge, sparsely covered with sagebrush and cedars; and before he showed himself Rover peered over the top and scanned the wide canyon below. They were moving up into the mountains whose high peaks, covered with snow, gleamed like crystal in the clear, morning air. There were cedar-brakes ahead, and tall pines in the distance; but the canyon was treeless and bare. Long and carefully Rover looked, then he spurred his lagging horse and led the way to the creek below.

Standifer saw a wide wagon-track, leading off up the gulch; and, just above the crossing, a wallowed place in the snow, which was blackened by a pool of blood.

"There it is," said Rover, jerking his thumb towards the spot, and Jeff reined over to look. Like reading an open book he saw where three men, all wearing boots, had roped and butchered a big steer. Then, leaving the offal for the coyotes to dispose of, they had loaded the carcass and moved on.

Circling wide to keep from tramping out the tracks, Standifer scouted for some sign of the hide and ears,

42

with their tell-tale marks of ownership. Then he stepped down and dug around beneath the ashes of their fire, but the rustlers had left nothing there.

"Must've taken the hide with 'em," observed Jeff at last. And Rover squinted at him dourly.

"I'll bet you the drinks from that bottle of mine," he said, "I can find the brand, right here."

"All right," agreed Standifer, after another look around; and Rover dropped off his horse.

"A Texas Ranger, hey?" he grumbled. "With lots and lots of experience. Look at that rock, you big lunkhead! Cain't you see it's been moved? Huh, huh—and he calls himself Good Eye!"

He strode down to the creek-bed and laid hold of a huge, flat boulder, which he heaved up with a scornful grunt.

"Now dig there," he directed, "while I take my drink. I'm something of a rustler, myself."

"So it seems," returned Jeff as, up from the half-frozen sand, he unearthed a patch of hide and two ears. "So that's the company's earmark—sharp the right and half-crop the left! And this is the Mill Iron brand!"

He spread out the strip of hide and surveyed it thoughtfully. "We call that the Equal O, back in Texas. It wouldn't be a hard iron to burn."

"You said it," grunted Rover enigmatically. "Or hair-burn, either, for that matter."

Standifer glanced up quickly but Rover's face was set like iron, though his eyes gave off a peculiar glint.

"I'll remember that," said Jeff and, knowing Rover's

43

vengeful nature, he surmised that he was hitting at Jack Flagg. In hair-branding, where part of the brand is seared into the flesh and the rest only burned into the hair, it is not until the calf sheds that the rustler can run his own brand. But hair-branding on a large scale can never be carried on without the knowledge and complicity of the range boss.

"I—see," nodded Standifer, after pondering the information. "Well, have another one on me, Rover, while I put these ears in my saddlebag. Now what's your idea on ketching these men?"

"I don't care if I do," responded Ralph the Rover amiably, giving the bottle another long pull. "Well, since you ask me, Good Eye—and since I've got a sneaking idee who this is—my advice is: Don't ride up on him while he's at work. He's kinder quick on the trigger and something like a grizzly bear, if you ever met one that had jest killed a cow. But after he's loaded his wagon and is riding home, half-froze, he might possibly listen to reason. Along towards evening, sometime. I believe you mentioned that you wanted to *arrest* him."

He drew his lip up sarcastically, but Standifer nodded.

"That's my system," he said. "And just to show you it can be done I'll pinch this man myself. So let's ride off the trail and get a little sleep. I don't suppose you've got anything to eat?"

"Not a bean," answered Rover. "But this whisky will do us—and come night we may get some of that beef."

He grinned again, sardonically, but Jeff let it pass; for after all his partner might be right. He knew the country and the people—even the man who had killed this steer—and to eat they might have to fight. Up a narrow side canyon, where their horses could paw down to grass, they lit a fire and dried out their saddleblankets. Then, muffled up in their greatcoats, they slept like the dead until the warmth of the brief day had passed.

Jeff was dreaming of hiding cravenly in the Bucket of Blood alley while bearded rustlers sought his life; and while he crouched there, starved and freezing, a ruthless hand laid hold of him and dragged him away to the hotel. He woke up, fighting desperately, to find Rover leaning over him and one arm in a vise-like grip.

"None of that, now!" warned Rover. "This don't call for no killing. All I want is that bottle of whisky."

He rolled Standifer over and fished out the bottle, which he had hidden in the folds of his overcoat, and with a sigh Jeff rose to his feet. The dream, at least, was over; and instead of facing Annabelle he had only to arrest three rustlers. He too took a drink, to start the blood in his veins, and in silence they took the trail.

Rover rode in the lead, his eyes scanning the ridges as they worked back into the hills; but the sun was sinking low before they sighted an abandoned camp, where the rustlers had killed another beef. Bits of meat lay by the fire, where they had cooked a hasty meal, and they snatched them up as they passed. The coals were still warm—and if they caught up with the loaded wagon there was no time to stop and eat.

Standifer spurred on ahead, like a hound on a fresh trail; while Rover, dawdling behind, ate wolfishly of the fragments and grinned at his partner's haste. Dusk had fallen in the woods and the wagon-track had lost itself as it fell into a well-used road; when through the trees ahead a sudden flame leaped up, and the officers came to a halt.

"They're lighting a fire," said Rover, "to warm up their hands. We're just in time—it's only three miles to Moab."

"You stay behind," ordered Jeff, "and we'll ride in on them, slow. And when we come in sight of the fire you ask for a drink, and I'll give it to you—maybe. But no shooting, now—this don't call for a killing. I'll attend to all three of them, myself."

"Go to it!" agreed Rover. "But don't forget about that drink. I believe I could stand one, right now."

"Nope—you've got to make a talk for it," answered Standifer. And they rode noisily off down the road.

A fire flared up before them, revealing a canvascovered wagon beside which stood three men, on their guard. Each held a Winchester, thrust out ready to shoot, but Jeff did not slacken his pace.

"Gimme a drink!" sang out Rover, beginning their play-acting; and as Standifer handed over the bottle he could see the three rustlers lower their guns.

"Now go easy on it," he warned, "and we'll give them a drink. And leave 'em to me," he muttered.

"Who's doing this?" demanded Rover, jerking away the bottle. "I bought that whisky, myself."

46

"Well, keep it, then," responded Standifer, spurring his horse towards the fire. And he glanced up at the rustlers from under his hat. Two stood back in the shadows, their guns held irresolutely; but the tall man who was their leader stepped forth into the firelight with his rifle ready to shoot, and still the Ranger kept on.

"By grab," he said, "that fire sure looks good!" And, dismounting awkwardly, he pulled his horse's head around and stepped to the ground behind him. Then swiftly from its holster, he whipped out his pistol and tucked it up the left sleeve of his overcoat.

"It's terrible cold," he complained, stumbling stiffly towards the fire; and the rustlers watched him; fascinated. Who it was they did not know, but he came on, his hands together, using his wolfskin sleeves for a muff; while his companion stopped to empty the bottle.

"Lord A'mighty," grumbled Standifer, feigning an ague of shaking as he hurried towards the warmth of the fire, it's cold—*ain't it?*"

He jerked the pistol out of his sleeve as he reached out his hands and rammed it into the tall leader's stomach, and suddenly his voice was hard.

"Drop that gun!" he commanded. "You're under arrest." But the rustler was too startled to resist. His hands went up, instinctively, and the two men behind him stood frozen in their tracks.

"I'll jest collect their hardware," spoke up Rover genially as he dropped nimbly down from his horse. "Fine weather for rustling, boys. Nice and cold—the meat will keep. Well, if it ain't Ike Cutbrush—from Moab!"

He stepped back in affected surprise and the tall rustler, swallowing his Adam's apple, suddenly burst into a fit of cursing.

"You Company spy!" he hissed. "I'll kill you fer this." But Rover only laughed.

"Have to ketch me first," he said. "And maybe break out of jail, to boot. This is Good Eye, the Texas Ranger."

CHAPTER VI
A Personal Favor

THERE WAS AN infinite pride in Ralph the Rover's voice as he announced the identity of his chief, but after another spell of cursing Ike Cutbrush applied his mind to the practical aspects of the case.

"A Texas Ranger, eh?" he sneered. "What's that got to do with me?"

"Well, besides that," explained Rover, "he's the new cattle detective that Cap Bayless sent back to Texas for. A cattle detective and a deputy sheriff. I'm a deputy sheriff, myself."

"Yes, you are!" laughed the rustler. "Why, it was only last week that you broke out of jail, yourself!"

"Never mind," returned Rover, turning vengefully to the wagon. "Now maybe you'll explain where you got this load of beef—and show the hides, as the law requires."

"Oh, certainly," mimicked Cutbrush, pulling down his long lip and turning to wink at his boys, "the hides are right under the seat."

Rover threw aside the canvas and fetched out three frozen hides. But when he spread them by the fire he found a hole where the brands had been and Cutbrush roared with laughter.

"Anything else you'd like to see? There's the heads, in the corner. Look 'em over—you might find the ears."

"Yes, and then again," observed Rover, "I might not."

"Well, what you going to do?" demanded Cutbrush of Standifer, as the earless heads were produced. "Go ahead now—prove I've killed Company beef!"

"You've killed somebody's beef, besides your own," returned Jeff, "or you wouldn't've cut out the brands. And when the case comes into court, Mr. Cutbrush, I'll try to produce the rest of my evidence. Rover, handcuff these gentlemen together and shackle them to a wagonwheel while we eat a few pounds of that beef."

"You'll play hell, shackling me," began Cutbrush belligerently, as Rover flashed his handcuffs; but when the new deputy started towards him he suddenly changed his mind and held out his wrists derisively.

"I'm onto your game," he said. "Trying to git me to resist, so you can beat me up, or kill me. Put your hands out, boys—they cain't prove nothing, nohow. And who ever heard of a man being convicted for stealing from the Mill Irons? They're the biggest

49

thieves of all. Didn't Jack Flagg and his cowboys rake Moab from end to end and drive off every cow-brute we owned?"

"He shore did!" replied his sons. And as Standifer started back for Bitterwater he pondered on what had been said. In a county where no man in fourteen years had been convicted on a charge of rustling, what chance was there, anyhow, of convicting this burly Mormon who now was so sneeringly defiant? And how could a Company which stole cattle itself—no matter under what provocation—ask a jury to return a verdict of Guilty?

He had made good his promise to Captain Bayless and arrested a notorious rustler. Ike Cutbrush was the butcher in the Mormon town of Moab, and the wagonload of meat which he had in his possession was intended to supply his shop. There were others, no doubt, who went out regularly and brought back Company beef; but why go through the mockery of arrest and trial, when no jury would ever convict? And there were other reasons, quite aside from the business at hand, why Jeff would do well to leave town. As he rode down the empty street and glanced up at the gallery where he and Annabelle had faced the crowd, he was thankful at least that she did not see him pass, and he left the prisoners with Rover.

When they came before the justice for their preliminary examination, brazenly confident of their instant release, Jeff had planned to produce the mangled brand and ears and make it an air-tight case. For no Judge, no matter how corrupt, would dare to let them go untried; and no Grand Jury, or petit jury either, could deny the authenticity of his proofs. He had the men, caught in the act of hauling off the beef. He had the hides of the animals and earless heads. And the cut-out brand and two severed ears would just fit back into place. It was a cinch, but Jeff could not stop.

"Lock these men up in jail," he said to Rover; and rode over to resign—or get fired. For by now the Captain would know.

There was a big horse at the hitching-rack in front of the Company House, and as Standifer admired the silver-mounted saddle he noticed the length of the stirrups. Only a man of great height and with tremendously long legs could fork a saddle like that. He glanced into the Captain's office and there, as large as life, he beheld Jack Flagg himself.

Jeff strode in arrogantly, throwing aside his wolfskin coat as if to invite attack, and Flagg jumped up with an oath. His head was heavily swathed in a bandage of white cloth, one of his eyes was blackened and bloodshot; but hate leaped from them both like a flame.

"Good evening, gentlemen," bowed Standifer; and Captain Bayless rose slowly to his feet.

"Mistuh Standifer," he said coldly, "this is Mistuh Flagg, my range boss."

"Yes, I've met the gentleman before," observed Jeff.

"By the gods, suh," burst out the Captain, after an apoplectic silence, "you think very well of yourself. But when I wrote Captain Ross for a trustworthy man I took it for granted he would send a gentleman. Can you explain why you struck Mistuh Flagg?"

"He was drunk," answered Standifer, "and tried to kiss your daughter, when I was escorting her to the hotel."

"What? Annabelle?" cried the Captain, taken aback. And Jack Flagg seemed to shrink and grow small. He glanced quickly from one to the other, reached uncertainly towards his gun, then whirled and strode out the door.

"Just a minute!" called Bayless, but he slammed out cursing with a last, stabbing glare at Jeff.

"Why, why—what's all this?" demanded the Captain, in a daze. "Is it true that you and Annabelle are married?"

"Well—yes," admitted Standifer, after a moment's silence. "Have you any objections, Captain?"

"Objections! Objections! What's the use of objecting? I sent her back East to keep her from marrying Jack—and now she has married *you!*"

"Yes, it's too damned bad!" answered Jeff, sarcastically. "But now that we're married I'm going to protect her—against her father, or Jack Flagg, or anybody. So I'll just turn in my report on this first arrest; and quit, before you fire me."

"What arrest?" barked the Captain, angrily.

"Ike Cutbrush and his two sons, for stealing beef. I've got them over in jail."

"Got the beef? Got the hide? Have you got the brand and ear-marks? You can't convict them without!"

"Yes, got everything," returned Standifer, "and here's the brand they cut out. They don't know I've got it—yet."

52

"I see," nodded Bayless. "You saved that for the Grand Jury! Have they admitted the possession of the hide?"

"Yes—to me. But I'm working for the Company, and my word might not count much in court."

"So you thought you'd let them admit it to the judge!"

The Captain was smiling now, in spite of his grouch; but Jeff stood grimly erect.

"That's the best thing to do," he advised. "I'm quitting the case, myself."

"What? Going to resign? I don't like this, Standifer!"

"I don't give a damn!" answered the Ranger desperately. "I've quit. You can get another man."

"But if I let you go now I'll lose my witness against Cutbrush, a man I've been after for years. Let's have a little drink and reconsider this, Jeff. By the gods, you're a credit to the Rangers!"

He slapped him on the back with such unaffected heartiness that Standifer was almost won over, but he shook his head and stood firm.

"Nope," he said. "Not if you feel that way about Annabelle. And if I stay I'll have trouble with Flagg. I'd better be going, Captain."

"Go if you must, my boy," sighed the Captain, as he filled up two glasses with Bourbon. "But to tell the truth, I'm beginning to like you. You remind me of the days when I was a Ranger myself, riding day and night after the Comanches."

He held up his glass and Jeff joined him in a drink,

though he kept one eye on the door. But the Captain would not let him go.

"Sit down!" he insisted. "I can see you are tired. Now tell me about your marriage to Annabelle."

He leaned back in his chair, his eyes twinkling expectantly, but Standifer only shrugged his shoulders.

"I'd rather not talk about it," he said.

"What? Trouble?" inquired Bayless. "Well, Annabelle is a nice girl. But willful, Mistuh Standifer—willful. She was spoiled by her mother, and spoiled by me—and this is the thanks we get. She has been in town two days and has not honored us with a visit. It's on account of her stepmother, of course." He sighed and glanced at Jeff, who sat in moody silence; sighed again and shook his head.

"But she must come to me," he said, "and ask my forgiveness. And she must ask the forgiveness of Mrs. Bayless."

"All right," agreed Standifer. "That's Annabelle's business. I'll just leave this brand, before I go."

He drew out a small package and placed it on the table, and the Captain regarded him fixedly.

"You're not going away?" he said at last. "I'm sorry, Jeff—truly sorry. But if it would make your stay any pleasanter, I'll never speak of Annabelle again. You've got your problem, I admit it, but why not work it out right here? And Jeff, I really need you on this case."

"This will cinch it," predicted Standifer, untying the package and spreading out the brand and ears. "And if

I stay here, Captain Bayless, Jack Flagg will either quit or—"

"Let him quit, then!" broke in the captain vehemently. "I swear I never thought that Jack would have the insolence to attempt to kiss my daughter in public. And for two days all I've heard from him is complaints about your conduct—without a word about the cause of it all. A man is justified, Mistuh Standifer, in protecting his wife—and if you go I'll never convict Cutbrush. He's a Mormon, and the Mormons stand together. They get their orders from the Bishop. And your man Rover has had trouble with Cutbrush—they'll claim it's all done out of spite."

"Well, have the district attorney challenge all the Mormon jurors, then."

"Fair enough—if we knew who they were. But there are hundreds and hundreds of Mormon sympathizers in the county, known only to the Bishop and the stake; and if they ever get one brother on that jury they'll acquit Ike Cutbrush, for a certainty."

"Does the Bishop," demanded Jeff, "stand in on this stealing? Does the Mormon Church justify rustling?"

"Well, no," returned the Captain, "the Church is against it. But these things happen, all the same."

"I'd like to go to that Bishop," spoke up Standifer impulsively, "and put him on record—yes or no. And then draw a jury of twelve straight Mormons and see what orders they got."

"By the gods, boy," cried Bayless, "I believe you've struck it! That is great! Simply grand! And Bishop Lillywhite, up at Moab, has always struck me as honest.

Couldn't you ride up and see him, Jeff?"

"Well, if it makes any difference," began Standifer reluctantly.

"It makes all the difference in the world," exclaimed the Captain. "And I'm really desperate, Jeff. If I don't stop this stealing it will ruin my fortune and drive the whole company into bankruptcy. But one conviction of a man as notorious as Cutbrush will mean the turning of the tide. I will consider it a favor—personally!"

He held out his hand and after a moment's hesitation Jeff weakened and gave him his own. But as he rode down the street past the Hotel Bitterwater he cursed himself for a fool. Dusk was falling, cold and windy, and the sidewalks were deserted; but on the gallery of the hotel a woman stood waiting, slim and beautiful in clinging grey furs. It was Annabelle, and she beckoned him in.

CHAPTER VII
Back in Texas

IT WAS TO AVOID meeting Annabelle that Jeff, with infinite pains, had timed his departure with the sun; but even at dusk she had been on the watch for him and as he looked up she smiled alluringly. Then, mysteriously, she beckoned him up; but Standifer motioned for her to come down. Her father had said that Annabelle was willful, but she met him as he stepped in the door.

She was enveloped in a cloak of soft, grey fur which set off her dark coloring and hair; and her eyes, which he had remembered as dancing with mischief, were big with hidden portent. Yet she smiled a glad greeting and, spying Mother Collingwood, Standifer relaxed the grim fixity of his lips. They were supposed to be married and, with others looking on, the least he could do was smile.

"Oh, Jeff!" she cried, "I've something to tell you. Have you got to leave town again?"

"Can't stop," he said, "except for a minute. Good evening, Mrs. Collingwood. How are you?"

"Oh, very well, thank you," replied the flustered looker-on. "You can use the best parlor, Annabelle."

She hurried off down the hall, as if remembering some errand, and Annabelle led the way and closed the door.

"They're all asking me questions—about my husband," she whispered tragically. "And I don't know a thing about you. Won't you sit down and tell me—Jeff?"

She glanced up at him so appealingly, and yet with such a smile, that he nodded and sank down on the plush davenport, which was reserved for the very elect. It was the last prized relic of those happy, bygone days when Mother Collingwood had had her own home.

"You're so tired!" exclaimed Annabelle sympathetically as she gazed into Jeff's windblown eyes. "Did you actually capture a cattle-thief? These women in the hotel are just afire with curiosity, and of course I had to tell them something! So I said you were a captain in the famous Texas Rangers. But you'll back me up—won't you, Jeff?"

"Sure! Sure!" he agreed. "But don't you think, Annabelle, we'd better tell them the truth, now?"

"Why, what do you mean?" she faltered.

"Well, about our not being married."

"Oh, hush!" she implored putting a finger to her lips as she tiptoed over to the door. "They're all crazy to find out," she explained, hurrying back. "I just know they'll be listening through the keyhole! So let's talk low, as if we were really married. And we can sit over here, in the corner."

"Suits me," agreed Jeff, moving over to the haircloth sofa; and she settled down beside him with a sigh.

"I've had such a time!" she confided. "Mother Collingwood is almost out of her mind—she just *knows* that something is wrong. But of course I couldn't tell her."

"Why not?" asked Standifer bluntly. "I just saw your father and—"

"Oh, you didn't tell him, did you?" she demanded. "My heart will just stop if Jack Flagg ever hears of this. Because I gave him my word—a year ago, when I went East—that the day I was eighteen I'd come back and marry him. And day before yesterday was my birthday!"

"My Lord!" breathed Jeff. "I begin to understand. But don't you think we ought to tell your father? It would help to square things, later."

"Oh, no! If he ever hears of it he'll begin all over

58

again to assert his paternal authority. And, Jeff, I'll simply die if I have to go back and be nice to that stepmother of mine!"

"Yes, but listen!" protested Standifer. "Can't you see how I'm fixed? These cowboys will kill me if they find out we're not really married!"

"Oh—shhh!" she cried, clapping her hand over his lips. "Now, Jeff, you must promise me, never to speak those words again. Because if you do, and somebody hears you—" She shuddered and glanced towards the door.

"I saw Jack!" she went on, as he sat in moody silence, "and his head was all wrapped up. But don't you know, Jeff, if I'd known who you were—I thought you were some city dude!"

She giggled ecstatically and Jeff had to laugh, though he wondered where Annabelle was leading him. They were strangers, or nearly so, and yet she still kept up the part which she had assumed when they left the train. But her glee over Flagg's plight was contagious.

"Yes, and so did Jack!" he grinned. "But I sure showed him different, with my six-shooter. But say, Annabelle, I'd better be going."

He rose up, to get the parting over quickly, but Annabelle clutched his hand.

"What? Now?" she gasped. "Why, you haven't told me anything! And don't you know that everybody is watching us? They'll just know that you're—not my husband!" she whispered in his ear. And Jeff felt himself persuaded, against his will.

"Well," he said, sitting down uncertainly and throwing aside his wolfskin coat, "what is it they want to know?"

"Why—everything!" she laughed. "Who you are and where you came from. And oh, yes—who is Rover?"

"He's a friend of mine," began Standifer, "and a mighty good friend, too. Kinder wild, you might say; but he was brought up wild—carried away by the Comanche Indians. They killed all his family and kept him for a slave—he was just a boy at the time—and ten or twelve years later they sold him up in Kansas, for two ponies and a sack of sugar.

"The trader asked him questions about his people and so on, but all he could remember was a dog with a curly tail that he'd played with when he was a child. And the name of this dog was Rover. Well, the trader wrote it down and put it in the papers, about this dog with the curly tail and so on, and some people back in Texas identified him by it and sent and brought him home. But by this time Rover was an Indian—all he would do was hunt and ride—and when his old uncle licked him he ran away and drifted West, and took the name of his dog. Said Rover was the only real friend he'd ever had and took the name out of spite. But he's a good pardner, if he likes you."

"Yes, but what was that he said about you being called Good Eye—and twirling your loop and all? Don't you remember? Down in front of the saloon?"

"Oh, that's an old joke of his," returned Standifer

easily. "We used to catch wild cattle together, and he's always making some crack."

"But the folks here all think you were rustlers together. Don't you remember he said you were called Good Eye, the Maverick King, because you could see them so far!"

"That's just an old gag," answered Jeff, "that he'd holler when he got good and drunk. And being as my eyes were better than most he hung the name on me. It's just like his taking the name of his dog. He's kinder peculiar, that way."

"I'm so glad," she sighed. "I'll tell that to Mother Collingwood. Because she thought, you know, that I'd married a regular cow-thief. It seems Rover isn't very well thought of."

"Well, they can take another think, then!" spoke up Standifer hotly. "He's the best pardner a man ever had. Of course he's run wild—throwed in with the wild bunch and probably got his full share of the mavericks. But I'd bank my life anytime on old Ralph the Rover. I got him appointed my deputy."

"So I heard," she nodded. "And oh, that reminds me—you *are* a Texas Ranger, aren't you? They all say you're nothing but a detective."

"Well, you tell 'em," he laughed, "that for once they're dead right. I'm nothing but a cattle detective."

"Why, Jeff!" she reproached. "After I've told Mother Collingwood you were a captain in the Texas Rangers!"

"I was a sergeant," he said, "if that will do you any good. But I had such good luck, cleaning up on a

61

bunch of rustlers, that Captain Ross advised me to specialize."

"Oh, goody!" she beamed. "I'll tell that to Mother Collingwood. I'm so glad you're not a common detective! Now tell me about that hat!"

"Oh, the cady!" he grinned. "That was only a bluff, in order to get into town. I didn't want any trouble—don't believe in all this fighting—so I passed myself off for a dude."

"What a story!" she mocked. " 'You don't believe in fighting!' Why, when you hit Jack and knocked him down with your gun I thought you were perfectly brutal!"

"Well, no harm done," he said. "If I hadn't done that I'd've had to kill him, maybe."

"And were you really so mad!" she inquired archly, "because he tried to steal that kiss!"

He glanced at her shrewdly and broke into a laugh. "Were you mad?" he asked, at last.

"Yes, I was!" she declared. "But you were a stranger and—and you said you'd explain it, sometime. Don't you remember you said: 'When a lady refuses a kiss—' But then you wouldn't go on."

"I was kinder excited, at the time," he said. "But you know, you were supposed to be my wife."

"So that was it!" she exclaimed, disappointed. "Well, I must say, you're not very gallant. I thought you were doing it for me!"

"Well, maybe I was, now," he admitted. "It was a kind of forced play, at the time. I warned the gentleman to leave you alone—"

"And then you hit him!" she pouted. "I nearly fainted."

"Yes, I noticed it," he answered. "That's why I took your arm—or maybe put mine around you."

"Oh, don't apologize!" she railed. "I don't hold it against you, although it does show you've had *some* practice. Tell me, Jeff—have you got a girl in Texas?"

She leaned over and gazed at him accusingly, and Jeff hesitated and scratched his head.

"Well, no," he said at last, "I reckon not. She *said* she was mine, but last time I heard from her she was going to marry some cowboy."

They both laughed together and Jeff rose once more to go, but she pulled him back insistently.

"And did you let her do it?" she demanded reproachfully. "After all your love-making and everything!"

"Yes, I did," he admitted. "You see, I'm a Ranger, and the Captain won't stand for married men. We're liable to get bumped off anytime, and it ain't quite fair to the widows."

"Do you mean?" she asked, "that you're likely to be killed now? Or are you just joking, Jeff?"

"Well, I'm something of a joker," he replied, "so don't take me too seriously, Annabelle. But this is a hard-game outfit that I'm up against now; and accidents, of course, will happen."

She stared at him, half frightened, as if the thought had never come to her that Standifer was playing with death, and then she took his hand.

"I'm sorry," she said, "that I got you into this. But

do you mind if I ask one more question? You see I'm all alone now, and of course I can't help thinking. You don't consider that we're married, do you?"

It was the question, he could see, which she had had in her mind when she had beckoned him into the hotel. A question which he himself had pondered while Ralph the Rover slept, and he had his answer pat.

"Not unless you do," he responded. And she started and let go of his hand.

"Why—Jeff!" she cried. "What do you mean?"

"That's all," he answered lightly. "Let it go the way it rides. Now what about Jack Flagg?"

"We were engaged," she murmured faintly. "I believe I told you that."

"Yes. A little late in the game—after I'd busted him over the head. But go on—I need to know."

"But why?" she protested. "It's all over, now."

"Then why," he countered, "is it necessary to keep this up, and pretend that we are married?"

"I'm afraid of him," she admitted, honestly. "You don't know him, Jeff—"

"Yes, I do!" he cut in. "I picked him out of the crowd. I knew he was there to kill somebody. He's a dangerous man, Annabelle, and I'm sorry I hit him. Now tell me what this is all about."

"Well, I wrote him," she confessed, "that I just couldn't marry him, and he wouldn't take No for an answer. So I bought me a wedding ring—" she showed it, on her finger—"and telegraphed ahead that I was married. I thought that would end it—and then, when the train stopped, I heard that big bull-fiddle!

64

And there was Jack, standing there, drunk! I realized right then I just *had* to have a husband or he would try to hold me to my promise. You were so nice to help me, Jeff."

She leaned her head confidingly against his shoulder and Standifer looked down at her, startled. Then he turned and glanced at the door. There was a flicker, and the keyhole showed clear again, and Annabelle drew away, blushing.

"Do you mind!" she asked, "if we pretend a little while? Just let them think you're my husband."

"Sure! Sure!" he agreed bluffly. "Anything you say, Annabelle. And here's something you can do for me. You tell these women that your husband is a detective and he's forbidden you to discuss his affairs. Who he is or where he came from, or anything about him. Because honest now, Annabelle, we're going to get into trouble if this news ever leaks out. Jack Flagg is sore already, and the first thing he'd do would be to grab a gun and come after me."

"Oh, I hadn't thought of that!" she gasped. "And they say he killed a man, back in Texas."

"Well, so did I," he answered grimly. And with a flash of white teeth he was gone.

CHAPTER VIII
The Bishop of Moab

THE SMILE DIED on Standifer's lips as he stepped out of the hotel and glanced up and down the street. He had not thought to linger so long with Annabelle, and there was a chance of getting shot from the dark. She had kept him against his will while his horse, at the hitching-rack, revealed his presence to his enemies; and yet, as he left, he glanced back into the lobby with a feeling that something was gone. Something that already haunted him, with sweet cadences and echoes of laughter—the voice and presence of a woman.

Her father had warned him that Annabelle was willful and he had set himself to resist her. But she had yielded to him in everything—and yet, as he looked back, he could see that she had had her way. How it came he did not know, but he had agreed to carry on the pretense of being her husband. Yet how could they hope, with an eye at every keyhole, to conceal what was obvious to all?

Falling into the joke of it, he had played along with Annabelle—pretending to be her husband, pretending that he supported her—until now he was caught in a jam. For if he admitted to the cowboys who, for all their *charivari,* were her admirers and devoted friends—if he admitted to one man that he was not Annabelle's husband, he would have a fight on his

66

hands. She was the belle of the town, in a country where women were scarce, and he knew all too well to what lengths they would go with a man who had compromised her name.

Though many of them were outlaws and fugitives from justice, drifted out to this last frontier, they had withal a stern sense of Western justice where the rights of a woman were involved. To steal a calf with them was no great breach of the moral code, since maver-icking was almost the rule on the range; but to steal a woman and boldly claim her as his wife would call for summary punishment. He even doubted his ability to put up much of a fight if Jack Flagg came riding for revenge.

Flagg had been beaten and humiliated and deprived of his girl by a man he had never seen, a man mas-querading as a hard-hatted Eastern dude, yet with a pistol up his sleeve. To what heights would his anger rise when he found that this strange man had no claim on the girl he loved? There was but one escape for Standifer, with his conscience and his honor clear, and Annabelle had barred the way. For if they admitted the hoax and he took the train East, then Jack Flagg would hold her to her promise. And Annabelle was afraid!

Jeff rode out into the murk of the wintry night, his head bowed in somber thought. If he let the play go on, posing weakly as Annabelle's husband, something worse was likely to happen. The girl would be dis-graced, his own good name blackened—and marriage would not help them, then. He had tried to cut the Gordian knot and go back to Texas, leaving Annabelle to explain away her prank; but her father had kept him on and some malign fate had left him like putty in her hands.

For a man in his right mind there were but two worthy solutions—an instant flight to Texas or an instant marriage with Annabelle. But how could he marry her, now? They were friends of a day, hurled together in a crisis, in which he had failed to play the leading hand. She had deceived him, inveigled him, led him aside from his purpose—and now she refused to confess. She was afraid! But how could he blame her, when he himself had failed to act the man's part? It was for him to take the lead and explain to her father, or offer to make amends; but some perverse happening always turned him from his purpose. It was as if the whole country were accursed.

From the moment he had set foot in it, stepping down off the train, a thousand devils had laid hold of him and led him such a dance that he doubted if it all was real. Had he accepted her, without thought, as his newly-wedded bride, and escorted her so blithely to the hotel? Had he signed his name and hers on the fatal register and given her money to pay? He had come there all set for a battle to the death, grimly determined to fight his way through, but he had ended on the gallery of the Hotel Bitterwater, making a speech as Annabelle's husband.

With a curse for his own supineness Standifer brushed the thoughts aside and rode up the Moab trail, but as the wind went down and he found himself nodding he turned out and built a fire. Then, while his horse fed and stamped, pawing away the light snow, he slept, still dreaming of Annabelle. But she was gay and joyous now, as he had seen her when she first crashed her star against his. Out of nowhere she had come, like a dazzling comet, and now their orbits were one. He was her man if not her husband, her protector and companion, and in his dreams all was happiness and life.

There was a halo that surrounded her, an aura of light and love that made her seem kin to the angels; and always, in his dreams, she was yielding and worshipful, and her head lay against his breast. She took his hand, she made much of him, she laughed at his jests; and her eyes sought his own like a child's. She was his, in his dreams, his to love and protect—but when he awoke he was cold.

His fire was dead and his horse, kicking and stumbling, had caught his hobbles in a snag. Jeff untangled him gloomily and built a fresh fire to take the chill out of his bones. Then in the stark and frosty silence he spurred on towards Moab, to beard the Mormon lion in his den. The road mounted upward, among ridges that grew higher until they broke off to the east in steep crags. A brook came brawling down, muddy with water from the thaw which had broken the long spell of cold, and in the distance plumes of smoke rose up. Then on the floor of a broad valley, divided off into checkerboards, the town of the Saints appeared.

Red brick houses, each by itself on a square of land, dotted the checkers like castles on a chessboard; and in the center, like a New England meetinghouse, rose the white-steepled Mormon church. Bearded men and towheaded children gazed out curious as he passed, for strangers were rare in Moab, but no one bade him welcome. They watched him, vacant-eyed or staring with suspicion, and Standifer rode on to the church. It was open now, ready for week-day school; the children stopped their play as he approached; and when he inquired for the Bishop's house a dozen hands pointed at once. But they too stared at him intolerantly.

It was a double house, made of brick, with two separate entrances to segregate the Bishop's two families; and at the rattle of the gate-chain the lord and master appeared, with a brood of staring children at his back. "Good morning, sir!" he hailed and stood waiting, big and dominating, as Standifer strode up the walk. At a glance he did not seem a man easily influenced or swayed one whit from his purpose. His hair and beard were red and his clean-shaved upper lip was set in censorious lines. Nor did his expression change when Standifer gave his name and mentioned that he was a deputy sheriff.

"Yes, sir!" challenged the Bishop. "And what can I do for you?"

"I want to talk with you," said Jeff, "about Ike Cutbrush and his sons. I'm the man who made the arrest."

"Oh, you are, eh?" returned the Bishop, his blue eyes lighting up with a gleam of fanatical hate. "Well, come in." And he opened the door.

They passed through a swarming hall into a wide front room where a woman was feeding a fire, but at a word from her husband she rose and went out and

Bishop Lillywhite closed the door.

"Sit down," he said, "and dry out your boots. It looks as if the spring thaw had come."

"I'm glad of it," answered Jeff. "I'm not used to much snow. Just came up from western Texas."

"I've heard of you," nodded the Bishop. "You're that new company detective that came up and arrested Cutbrush."

"That's right," agreed Standifer. "And I'd like to know, Bishop, how the Mormon Church stands on this rustling."

"The Church of Latter Day Saints," roared Lillywhite, "is absolutely opposed to it, as it is to all forms of crime. It stands for a strict morality and a respect for every law, no matter what others may say."

"So I've heard," responded Jeff. "And since I happened to arrest Ike Cutbrush I thought I'd better consult you."

"Why, me," bellowed the Bishop, "instead of somebody else? I'd like to inform you, Mister Deputy Sheriff, that Ike Cutbrush is not a Mormon. He has refused to pay his tithings or attend the church meetings, and the same holds true of his boys."

"All right," began Standifer, "now here's how it stands. I arrested these three men with a wagonload of beef which they had killed on the open range. They had the hides and they had the heads, with the ears cut off. But, Mr. Lillywhite, I've got those ears."

"You have?" repeated the Bishop, and his face subtly changed. He stopped roaring, and Standifer smiled.

71

"Yes, sir," he said, "and I've got the brand, too, that they cut out and hid under a rock. They don't know that yet, but I'm telling it to you. Now here's what I want to know. If we bring this case to trial and prove beyond a doubt that Cutbrush is guilty of rustling, can I depend upon this Church—of Latter Day Saints, as you call it—to help me get a conviction? Captain Bayless says I cannot."

"Well, you tell Captain Bayless," began the Bishop acrimoniously, "that he doesn't need to worry about *us*. There are some, like Ike Cutbrush, who bring discredit on the Saints by stealing their neighbors' cattle. But for every cow they take, Jack Flagg and his cowboys steal back a hundred more."

"A hundred?" echoed Jeff, and Lillywhite slammed his fist down.

"Yes, a hundred! And even more!"

"Well, who gets these cows?" began Standifer cautiously. "Excuse me, but I'm kinder curious."

"Yes, and well you may be, if you're only a newcomer in the country. I don't doubt that Captain Bayless and his range boss, Jack Flagg, have filled you up with lies about my people. But I tell you, Mr. Standifer, that cattle have been stolen from us and branded over to the Company. They may lose, and I think they do, a great many steers; but that is no excuse for robbing honest ranchers who are struggling to make a living."

"Certainly not!" agreed Jeff. "But this is the first news I've had that Jack Flagg and his cowboys are stealing. In fact, Captain Bayless told me that unless the rustling was stopped the Company would go into bankruptcy. Now who is it that gets these cows?"

"The Company!" answered Lillywhite. "And then the cowboys turn around and steal them back for themselves."

"Aha!" nodded Standifer. "Now we're getting down to cases. But can you prove that, Bishop Lillywhite, in court?"

"That is not my business," returned the Bishop stiffly. "But I know it, beyond the peradventure of a doubt. It was only last year—just before he was fired—that Jack Flagg and his round-up crew raked this valley from end to end, driving off every cow-brute they found. Even our milk-cows and sucking calves were taken out of the pasture and branded into the Mill Iron brand."

"Well," suggested Jeff provocatively, "perhaps that's the reason Flagg was fired."

For a moment the Bishop surveyed him scorn-fully—then he broke into a laugh.

"Well, you *are* new!" he said. "Jack was fired right after the round-up, for making love to the boss's daughter. And the reason Bayless hired him back was—he couldn't get along without him! His own cowboys were stealing right and left."

"I can believe that," nodded Standifer, "because I've never known it to fail. When a big Company goes to stealing, its own men will steal back from it—as much or more than they took. The only way to stop rustling is to stop all rustling. I won't work for an outfit that steals."

73

"Then you'd better resign," advised the Bishop. "The Mill Iron has been mavericking for years. Why do you think the Company puts its men out in these winter camps, if not to run their brand on every calf? That's their duty—range-branding—only they're not very particular whose brand it is they run. When Jack Flagg quit, all these line-riders and winter-camp men set out to feather their nests. And unless I'm mistaken Jack Flagg himself branded more than any of his men.

"Is that so?" exclaimed Standifer. "What brand does he run?"

"I don't know," snarled Lillywhite. "That is something that doesn't concern me. But this I do know— we never got back our cows. And the sheriff refused to make any arrests."

Jeff rubbed his nose as he pondered the significance of all that the Bishop had said. And yet it did not come wholly as a surprise. As a cattle detective he had found the same conditions on almost every range he worked. Big men stealing from little men, and the little men stealing back—and sooner or later it was the big Companies that lost and sent out a call for help. Yet it did not seem reasonable that an old Ranger like Captain Bayless would permit such a wholesale round-up.

"Do you think?" he inquired, "that Captain Bayless stands in on this? Or is the stealing done without his knowledge?"

"He's being robbed by his own men," stated the Bishop firmly. "I consider the old Captain an honest man."

"Well!" exclaimed Standifer, brightening up. "Then

74

perhaps we can get together. Because that's just what he said about you."

"He's honest," repeated Lillywhite impersonally, "but he trusts his men too far. Now what can I do for you, my friend?"

"Do you want to stop this rustling?" demanded Jeff.

"Yes, I do!" affirmed the Bishop. "But I want to stop it all. And it seems a little unusual that the first man arrested should be Ike Cutbrush and his sons. It looks like persecution, and my people have suffered enough. But at the same time, if they're guilty I will favor their conviction—*provided* you don't stop there!"

"I get the point," nodded Standifer, "and I'll tell you what I'll do. You show me a Gentile, or a Company man either, that I can catch stealing a Mormon's cow, and I'll arrest him and put him through."

"The Mormons have lost their cows," returned the Bishop, grimly. "And besides, no jury would convict. In fourteen years there hasn't been a single conviction, so why invite the wrath of our enemies?"

"Well, now, I've heard," countered Jeff, "that the Mormons are the ones to blame. The sheriff himself says he can't convict a Mormon rustler, no matter how guilty he's proved. He says they always get one man on the jury, and they'll hang it, every time."

"No, and he can't convict a Gentile, or anybody else!" raged Lillywhite. "The cow-thieves who have been acquitted have not all been Mormons, nor are they the principal offenders. It is a well-known fact that most of the Texas cowboys, who were brought into this country by the Company, have set up in business for themselves—and their sympathies are all with the rustlers. Of course they blame every acquittal on the Mormon members of the jury, but the whole community is against the Mill Iron Outfit. And do you know why? Because the Company itself is the biggest thief of all!"

The Bishop slammed one fist into his brawny left hand, but Standifer shook his head.

"Not if it's going into bankruptcy," he said. "Somebody else is getting more than they are."

"Well, it's Jack Flagg and Bill Longyear, then, and all that gang of Texans. You can see that this valley is stripped. The Mormons have lost, from the start."

"Yes, and they'll keep right on losing," predicted Jeff, "until the last of this rustling is stamped out. That's my job, Mr. Lillywhite, and I intend to do it, but right at the start I need a little help. You say the Church is opposed to stealing and you're for convicting Ike Cutbrush if he's guilty? I'm going to give you a chance now to go on record in this matter, since Cutbrush is considered to be a Mormon. I will ask the district attorney for a jury of twelve Mormons, and we'll just see if they turn him loose."

He rose up smiling and after a long, hard stare the Bishop held out his hand.

"Very well," he said, "I will use my influence to see that a just verdict is rendered. But when I report, as I may, some Gentiles who are stealing—"

"I'll get them," promised Standifer, "or they'll get me. I'm here to stop all rustling."

"Well and good," nodded the Bishop. "The Church

will do its share. But, young man, don't forget your promise."

CHAPTER IX
On Being Honest

SPRING WAS GLEAMING in the air when back from the mountains, Standifer splashed across the muddy ford. The Little Colorado was a river again instead of a glaze of ice; and out on the flats the cattle stood motionless, drinking in the warmth of the sun. Winter had broken and the day was approaching when the Mill Iron round-up would begin. For with the sun would come green grass, and cows lowing for their calves, and bands of horses, scouring the plains. Even Bitterwater had awakened to new life.

A row of cow ponies stood waiting outside the Company Headquarters while their masters drew supplies at the commissary; the big corral behind was astir; but as Jeff glimpsed Annabelle walking gaily down the sidewalk his heart sank, and the glory was gone. The death's-head of a new fear rose up before him, making him rein in and keep out of sight. For the dearly beloved pretense could go on no longer. He must quit now and get out of town.

She went on, unconscious of his presence, until she passed into the New York Store; and then, suddenly grim, he rode by without stopping and dropped his reins at the Company horse-rack. Captain Bayless was busy now, making out checks and requisitions; but at sight of Standifer he brushed them all aside and reached into the locker for his bottle.

"Well, well, my boy," he said, with a benevolent smile. "Sit down and we'll have a drink. Isn't this weather simply wonderful? A typical Arizona day! It won't be a week till we have grass."

"Looks fine," admitted Jeff as he went through the familiar ceremony with which the Captain opened and closed all business; and for a moment he was tempted to speak out. To confess to her father Annabelle's harmless prank and the complications that were bound to ensue. But no, the way out was to leave town for-ever—for Annabelle was afraid of Jack Flagg.

"Well, what news?" demanded Bayless. "How's my old friend, the Mormon Bishop? Did he fall in with your plans?"

"Yes," answered Standifer, "he practically agreed to instruct the brethren to cinch Cutbrush. Provided," he went on, "we work just as hard to get the first Gentile he reports."

"That's reasonable," conceded the Captain, "you must have put up quite a talk, Jeff. The Mormons have been hostile of late."

"Yes. It seems your round-up crew went through Moab last spring and took every cow they had. Even the milk cows and sucking calves—and branded them into the Mill Iron."

As Jeff went on with the Bishop's complaint, Bay-less leaned back and plucked angrily at his goatee.

"That's enough!" he interrupted. "The Bishop failed to mention the number of Company cows that we

78

found. And how many white-faced calves we found sucking Mormon cows—two and three, in fact, to a cow. So Jack simply made a clean sweep of the Valley, to show them that such tactics don't pay. He's hot-headed, I'll admit it, but absolutely honest. And if he ever stole a cow, it was for the Company, not himself. I checked up on his brand after I discharged him last spring, and he had a cow for every calf. Now that's being honest, for a range boss, that could steal me blind if he wanted to—and he's the only man that can handle those cowboys. When I fired him and hired old John Dobbins I lost a thousand calves, easy."

"Well, all right," drawled Jeff, "if that's what you call honest. But you and Jack Flagg will have to get more honest, if you ever expect to convict Cutbrush. The only way to stop stealing is to stop all stealing—and the Company will have to quit first. Otherwise no jury will convict."

"What—what?" exploded the Captain, "are you criticizing our methods? I was in the cattle business, suh, before you were born and I reckon I've learned the first principles. You can't exist in a rustler country, with everybody pulling from you, if you don't pull a few yourself!"

"Maybe not," stated Standifer, "but I've seen some big Companies go bust by applying those principles. Because the minute the Company steals, or goes to hogging the mavericks, every little man in the country is out with the long rope—and the cowboys worst of all. If you hire a man to steal, or range brand for the Company, if he's got the brains of a rabbit he'll set up in business for himself. Now I may be wrong, Captain, but in my opinion that's just what has happened, right here."

"But—but how can you remedy it?" demanded Bayless, after a pause. "By the gods, Jeff, you may be right."

"You'll have to work fast," admitted Jeff. "But the way to begin is to get religion yourself—and then put the fear into their hearts. Tell your cowboys to quit pulling and see that they do it. Then round up these rustlers until the jail is jam-full. That's my way, and it's worked with bigger outfits than this. But if you don't like it, of course I'll quit."

The Captain reached over and rang a silver bell and as his aged colored servitor appeared he ordered him to summon Jack Flagg. Then he waited, drumming his fingers and staring out the door, until suddenly the range boss strode in.

At sight of Jeff he stopped in his track, but Bayless jerked his head, impatiently.

"Come over here, Jack," he said. "I've been talking with Mistuh Standifer about how to stop this rustling. And now I want your opinion."

"That ain't my business," answered the range boss, evasively. "Keeps me busy running the line camps, and wagons."

"Well, it's my business," replied the Captain, "and I'm going to stop it, too, if I have to ride the range, myself. I'm going to stop it, Jack, if I have to fire every cowboy and send back to Texas for gunmen. I've got to stop it, or I'll lose my last dollar and the

Company will go out of business."

"All right," returned Flagg, with a note of challenge in his voice. "Go ahead and stop it, Captain."

"I'll begin," blared Bayless, "by giving you my orders, which I expect you to carry out. I want you to instruct every man on our payroll not to brand a single maverick or sleeper. And more than that, I want this pulling to cease—and particularly from the Mormons around Moab."

"Stop right there!" broke in Flagg, his eyes red with anger. "I can see what you're leading up to, and I know who put you up to it. So you can take your choice, here and now—either get a new range boss or a new stock detective. Because this man and me can't hitch." He cast a fleeting glance at Standifer, who returned the look with interest. "He's just out to make trouble," declared the range boss, vehemently. "So let's come to a show-down, right now."

Jeff sat motionless and unruffled in his chair, waiting expectantly for the Captain to speak. At last the time had come when he could give up his position and drift silently out of town, but Bayless did not respond at once.

"That's all right," said Standifer, evenly. "Don't mind my feelings, Captain—I can see we'd never get along. And since it's easier to get a detective than it is a good range boss I'll just quit and let you catch your own rustlers."

He rose up smiling and Jack Flagg bristled back at him, his teeth bared in a triumphant grin; but Bayless held up his hand.

"Just a minute!" he commanded peremptorily. "Don't take too much for granted, young man. I'm sorry, Jack, but I'll have to let you go."

"Who—me?" demanded Flagg, taken aback. "Well, who'll run your wagons, Captain? Can this tinhorn detective do it? The boys will all quit, to a man!"

He paused, panting, his face white with rage.

"Let them quit!" returned the Captain. "I've thought this all out. If I can't keep my calves, what's the use of branding them? And if I can't get a range boss that will co-operate to stop this rustling—"

"All right!" snarled Flagg, and turned on his heel. But as he started for the door Standifer made a last bid for freedom.

"Oh, hell!" he scoffed. "I don't want the damned job. I've got a better one, back in Texas, where the folks are more my style. I just came out here to accommodate Captain Ross."

Flagg had stopped at the door to listen, and at Standifer's words he stared. Then a grin of sly cunning spread over his face and he came back, teetering on his toes.

"Oho!" he said, "so that's what's biting you? You're afraid, Mr. Bad Man from Texas! Well, it's a danged good thing you are, because these rustlers will shore git you if the honest cowboys don't beat 'em to it. We don't approve, none of us, of the *way* you treat your wife—and I've heard you've been a rustler, yourself. A damned good rustler—so good they named you Good Eye! But you've played out your string in Bitterwater."

He swaggered up closer, swaying top-heavily in his high boots, and stopped to hook his thumb in his belt. "You don't look bad to me, at all!" he announced. "If you don't get out of here, I'll kick you out."

"No you won't," cut in Bayless. "And Jack, you've been drinking, or you'd never talk that way to Jeff. He was a sergeant in the Texas Rangers, under my old friend, Captain Ross—and no Ranger was ever kicked out."

"Not by a damned, drunken cowboy, with his head tied up in a rag," taunted Jeff as he stood his ground. "Take that hand away from your gun!"

He paused and at the challenge Jack Flagg withdrew his thumb, passing it off with a knowing leer.

"All right," he said, "I'm onto your game. You can't cap me into no gun-fight. The boys will take care of your case."

"Think so?" retorted Standifer. "Well, I'll tell you what I'll do, then. I'll just stay, and give them a chance. And as for you, Mr. Flagg, just to show you what I think of you—you hold your job and I'll hold mine and we'll see who weakens first."

"I'll go you," agreed Flagg, "if only to show you up." And he strode out the doorway, grinning.

CHAPTER X
An Indian

A COLD, KILLING light had crept into Standifer's eyes as he bandied words with Jack Flagg. His reason told him to refrain but some primitive impulse tipped his tongue with words of fire. He had baited him purposely, to draw him into a fight and decide their grudge then and there, but Flagg had sensed his danger and drawn back. And as he went out the door he was grinning.

"What's the joke?" demanded Jeff, as he met the Captain's glance; but Bayless shook his head.

"Don't ask me," he sighed. "But Jeff, my boy, you told me you were not a killer. I remember, when I hired you, you spoke at some length on the peaceful methods you employed."

"This is different," declared Standifer stubbornly. "Did you hear what he said—about the way I treat my wife? That's what's behind all this."

"Nevertheless," insisted the Captain, "that is not a sufficient reason for deliberately seeking to kill him. Jack is a good man, Mistuh Standifer, except when he's drinking. And of course, he was fond of Annabelle."

"He's crazy about her, yet," stated Jeff. "That's why he wants to kill me. But, drunk or sober, he hasn't got the nerve; and a man like that gets dangerous. The next thing he'll do will be to shoot me from behind.

That's the reason I tried to jump him out."

"No, no, my boy," protested Bayless earnestly. "You don't understand Jack's nature. He's intensely loyal to his friends—and in this country they number thousands. When he spoke about Annabelle it merely reflected his solicitude—a solicitude which I share, myself. You mustn't take this so hard."

"Well, you tell him from me," warned Standifer, "to leave Annabelle strictly alone. As long as she's my wife I'll protect her good name—and how I treat her is none of his business. Now what about it—am I fired?"

"Certainly not!" declared the Captain, "though I couldn't help wondering if I was still General Manager of the Mill Irons. You boys took it away from me and hired and fired yourselves so fast that I felt like a mere outsider."

"You can fire me again, if you want to," answered Jeff. "I'm not so stuck on the job. But if I stay, Captain Bayless, this Company stealing must stop. I want a letter from you, instructing every Mill Iron cowboy to follow the rules you laid down. No riding the range for mavericks, or running off neighbors' calves, or dealing these Mormons misery."

"You shall have it," stated Bayless. And, writing it out, he signed his name with a flourish.

"There, my boy," he said, "go and show that to the Bishop; and tell him I stand behind it."

"All right," agreed Jeff, "and then I'll visit your winter camps and show it to some of your cowboys."

"Very well," assented the Captain, shortly. "And

after that—what then?"

"I'll rake your range from one end to the other, rounding up these rustlers and long-ropes. I'll jam that jail so full they'll be sleeping three deep—and every man caught in the act."

"That sounds good!" smiled Captain Bayless. "But can you do it alone—or with the help of that drunkard, Rover? He went on a tear the day you left town and he's been on it ever since."

"I'll take him out of town," promised Standifer. "There'll be no more trouble from him."

"But I hesitate, my dear boy, to let you undertake this task with no one to assist you but Rover. Jack gives him a very bad name—it seems the man is part Indian."

"He's all Indian," answered Jeff, "if you try to run it over him, or fill him up on forty-rod whisky. But Rover is my old compadre and I'd stake my life on him any time. And if he's been associated with these rustlers, as he probably has, that makes him all the more valuable.

"The thing to do, now, Captain, is to keep the Bishop in line until we can get a conviction on Cut-brush. So if I can catch a couple of Gentiles, or a Mexican or two, before the Grand Jury sits, it will clear the atmosphere wonderfully. All I ask of you is to watch the district attorney, and the sheriff and all the rest of them, while I fill that jail up with rustlers. I'll be back in about a week."

He touched his hat briefly and strode out the door before the Captain could offer him a drink. And then, out in the street, he suddenly remembered Annabelle. She would be watching for him, on the gallery of the hotel. He had burned his bridges behind him and there was no retreat; but what could he say to her, now? Riding slowly down the street his eyes scanned the vacant gallery where before she had waited and watched, but Annabelle was nowhere to be seen. Then a loud shout of triumph from the Bucket of Blood diverted his thoughts from their course and pushed through the swinging doors.

Ralph the Rover was winners in the faro game, which he always bucked best while drunk, and he only glanced up at Jeff.

"Copper the queen to lose," he orated. "Another ten on the jack. And, dealer, draw the cards from the top."

He watched the game intently, changing his bets as the odds changed, and whooped again as he called the last turn.

"That's luck," he declared. "You stay right with me, Jeff, and I'll bet you we break the bank. Here, hold my roll for me, pardner."

He gathered up a big sheaf of bills and thrust them into Standifer's hands, and then the game went on. It dragged slowly for Jeff, but he could not escape, not even to get a lunch at the stand. With drunken insistence Rover kept him at his side and no arguments would persuade him to quit.

"No!" he hollered. "What? Quit while you're winning? You quit your luck and your luck will quit you. Stay with me, and we'll break the bank."

Night fell and in the lamplight the battle continued.

Then a new dealer came on and subtly the luck changed. Rover lost, but played doggedly on. Jeff sequestered part of his winnings, the quicker to get it over with, and always in his mind he had a picture of Annabelle—and his horse, standing in front of the saloon. Should it be told around town that he had stopped at the Bucket of Blood while his wife watched and waited next door? And what would Annabelle think?

"Now, here!" he said at last, breaking in on Rover's maunderings. "I've got something else to do besides sit here and watch you lose. Take your roll, and sluff it off, quick."

He started for the door, but Rover rushed after him and dragged him back to the bar.

"Jest one drink," he implored, "for old time's sake and, Good Eye, we'll hit the trail!"

"Well, stay here and drink it," answered Standifer shortly. "I'll be back in half an hour."

"I'll go with you," volunteered Rover generously. "Because I know just where you're going. You're going to see your wife."

"Shut your blathering mouth!" burst out Jeff in a fury. "Do you think I'd go back to her, drunk?"

"W'y, you ain't drunk!" protested Rover.

"Well, with *you,* then!" snapped Standifer, "as drunk as a fool. Come on, let's get out of this hole."

"If you're too damned good to associate with me," began Rover with offended dignity, "you can go to hell in a hand-basket! Here, take your old star and get another man—I'm going back to break that bank."

"No you're not," spoke up Jeff, laying hold of him resolutely, "you're coming with me, right now. My wife is so mad by this time she wouldn't speak to me, anyway." And he dragged Rover out the door.

There were struggles, and maudlin arguments, as he put Rover on his horse; and above him in the darkness Jeff was conscious of Annabelle, looking down from the gallery of the hotel. He had a sinking feeling that the end of their friendship had come, the end to all his hopes and dreams; but perhaps it was all for the best. It *was* for the best, for Rover was drunk—and sooner or later the dreams must end. But oh, how people would talk!

CHAPTER XI
The Rustler Yell

FOR TWO DAYS, sullenly and in Indian silence, Ralph the Rover led the hunt for rustlers. He rode south and then east through a country covered with pines, with wide glades and rugged canyons between, but it seemed as if their movements were watched. They came upon a maverick, freshly branded into the Hog Eye, the iron of Hog Eye Bill Longyear; but the Rustler King was nowhere to be seen. Nevertheless they took the tip that he was watching them and circled far to the east, quitting the trails and travelling by night. It was a grim and silent business, with nothing to drink and little to eat, and in the end Rover found his tongue.

"This is Mexican country ahead," he said, waving his hand towards some rough, timbered ridges. "They call it Spanish Peaks. Nothing to eat but beans and *chili con carne*—how'd you like a little white man's grub?"

"Suits me," responded Standifer indifferently, "as long as they don't spot us for officers."

"Oh, this old Colonel Rhubottom is so far behind the times he don't know that Lee has surrendered. He lives up yon canyon, where that lava rim shows, and he's honest as the day is long."

"The days are awful short, now," observed Standifer cynically; but Rover was not to be denied.

"And grub!" he exclaimed. "I never seen the time when he didn't have lashings of everything. Plenty of beef, lots of coffee with real cream, straight from the cow—the finest bread and cake you ever et. The old man is from Kentucky and keeps a jug of the best. I can taste that liquor, right now."

He smacked his dry lips and reined into the trail and Standifer decided to humor him.

"Go ahead," he said, "and if we don't get the drink we may ketch him butchering a beef. There's sure somebody in these parts doing an awful lot of hair-branding, and that don't look like Mexican work."

"I'll show you some Mexican work—tomorrow," promised Rover. "There's a snaky bunch over in them peaks. But before I have a battle with a gang of Greasers I want a good drink under my belt."

He led the way up a dark canyon where the over-hanging rimrock cast black shadows into the valley below; but the Colonel was absent from his log cabin among the pines and the womenfolks were frightened and shy. Nothing was said at the frugal board, and supper that night was corn-pones and blue, skimmed milk. Jeff doubted if they were really welcome. For breakfast they had the same—no beef and no coffee— and Rover rode away in a pet.

"Dang his heart!" he grumbled, "the old colonel seen us coming and tuk out into the rocks. I found his tracks, down by the barn. He's heard the news somehow—and he tuk that jug with him. I looked around for it, everywhere."

"Yes, I saw you," answered Jeff. "And the old lady saw you, too. You might say, in fact, she was watching you. But say, wasn't that beef we had fine! And the coffee—with real cream, straight from the cow! And that riz bread and cake! I'm plumb spoiled for Mexican cooking!"

"Aw, you think you're smart as hell!" yapped Rover. "As if a man never made a mistake. You've been beefing and complaining about everything I do. Now you cut the wind, for a change. Jest lead me to some house where the people will make us welcome, and set out the company beef. I'm burnt out on being the goat."

"All right," agreed Jeff, spurring his horse up in front. "It's a cinch I can't do any worse. You've showed me lots of country, and lots of pisen mean settlers that made signal-fires on the buttes when we left. But that isn't what we came out for. I want to ketch some cow-thief, to keep Ike Cutbrush company, so we'll head over into these Spanish Peaks."

He reined his horse out of the trail and crossed the country at random, shaking his rope out as he rode. When a cow and calf jumped up he took after them on the run, following their dust wherever they led; and so on, in rustler fashion, until they came out at last at the head of a broad, open valley.

"Now look out, you danged fool," warned Rover from behind, "you're crowding into Mexican country. The first thing you know you'll run against a bullet— these *paisanos* don't like Company men, at all."

"Fair enough," returned Jeff. "Because I don't like Mexicans. There's a house, away down there in that swale."

He pointed, and Rover narrowed his eyes down intently.

"There's some Mexicans," he said at last.

"Six of 'em," counted Standifer. "And I'll bet you ten dollars they've hung up a Mill Iron beef."

"Beef—nothing!" scoffed Rover. "That don't cause no excitement. Look at them *hombres,* huddling up."

"They've seen us," stated Jeff. But Rover snorted. "They have not," he contradicted. "They've got a bottle of mescal, I'll bet you dollars to doughnuts."

"Well, in that case," grinned Jeff, "you ought to be game to ride down there. Let's whirl in on 'em, before they can hide."

"Go to it," answered Rover, loosening his gun in its scabbard; and they charged down the long, narrow trail.

The house stood backed up against the edge of a dry wash, with a second house, half hidden, behind. And across the wash, to the east, there rose the steep bank of a mesa. Clumps of scrub-oak crowned its top but, except for scattered pines, there was little to impede the view.

As they loped down out of the brush and headed straight across the flat the six Mexicans turned to watch them. Then one by one they drifted away behind the house, leaving their leader to face the two cowboys. He was afoot, and unarmed; but as they rode up closer Jeff could see he was a dangerous man. His skin was almost white, showing his Spanish blood; his deep-set eyes never wavered; and beneath the shadow of his thin, drooping moustache his thick lips drew back scornfully.

"Good morning, sir," he hailed in perfect English as Jeff reined in before him. "Who are you, and what do you want?"

"We are officers," answered Standifer, "out looking for stolen beef; and I'd like to search your house."

"Very well, sir," returned the Mexican. "This is my house. You may search it. But how do I know you are deputy sheriffs, and not a couple of cow-thieves, your-selves?"

He spoke up boldly, but Jeff did not argue with him.

"You don't," he said. "Rover, go in and search that house. The one behind is padlocked."

He sat his horse in the open, one eye on his prisoner, the other on the mesa beyond; and Rover came out with two guns.

93

"That's all," he reported; and the Mexican eyed him malignantly.

"Those are my guns," he stated angrily.

"I'll keep 'em for you," mocked Rover. "Now, where's the key to that house?"

He pointed to the log cabin which stood in the rear, its door fastened by a padlock and heavy chain. Smoke was curling from the chimney, showing it had lately been occupied, but the five men who had been there were gone.

"That is the home of my brother-in-law," said the Mexican. "Unless you have a warrant for him, or a search warrant, you have no right to enter his house."

Standifer looked him over appraisingly. He was surprisingly well educated, for a Mexican—or at least regarding the right of search. And, of course, Jeff had no search warrant.

"Where is your brother-in-law?" he asked.

"He has gone down the valley, with his friends," returned the Mexican; and his eyes took on a sinister gleam. Jeff glanced down the canyon and saw the dust of their flight, and broad sombreros bobbing as they rode. Then he turned and reached into his coat.

"Here is my search warrant," he said, fetching out the official envelope which contained his deputy's commission. But the Mexican, as he had guessed, could not read English. He eyed the stamps and seals, holding it upside down, then handed it sulkily back.

"I don't give a damn!" he shouted roughly. "You can't go inside that door."

"Take that axe, Rover," directed Jeff, "and chop the

door open. I'll bet you we find some beef."

He shifted in his saddle, bringing the muzzle of his pistol in line with the cursing Mexican, and waited while Rover swung the axe. The chain could not be broken, nor could the padlock be smashed, so he hacked a hole through the door-jamb and finally jerked the door open.

"Fresh beef," he announced, peering cautiously in; and then he darted inside. Jeff gave over for a moment his close watch on the Mexican, and Rover came bounding out.

"It's a Mill Iron steer," he began; and then he looked wildly around. "Hey!" he yelled. "Where the hell is that Mex?"

Standifer turned to where, but a second before, the Mexican had been sullenly eyeing him; but like a flash he had disappeared.

"I'll get him," he said, jumping his horse around the corner; and a hundred yards away, across the wash, he beheld the Mexican, running for the mesa.

"Halt!" ordered Standifer, jerking his rifle out of its scabbard; and Rover came running after him.

"Kill the scoundrel!" he yelped as the Mexican kept on. "You've ordered him to halt! Now bore him!"

"Leave him to me!" answered Jeff, galloping down the low bank and out across the broad wash below. "Hey! Halt!" he called again; but the Mexican ignored him, bounding up the steep bank like a buck. Standifer rushed his horse after him, grimly determined to ride him down, equally determined not to shoot an unarmed man; but as he started up the bank his horse slipped and stumbled, falling back in a shower of stones.

Jeff dropped off and grabbed one rein, snaking his reluctant mount after him, until at last they scrambled up the rim. The level top of the mesa was covered with scrub oaks and through them, running hard, the desperate Mexican plowed his way, paying no attention to his pursuer. Standifer shouted, then threw the spurs into his dispirited horse and hit him over the rump with his gun-barrel. They gained by leaps and bounds, but just as they ran up on him the Mexican plunged out of sight. He had crossed the high mesa and started down the opposite bank towards a wooded bench beyond.

In a storm of sticks and dirt Standifer whipped down after him, saying nothing but with his gun raised to strike. Something told him that the Mexican was leading him into an ambush, laid perhaps by the men who had fled. Otherwise he would stop, to escape being shot, or double and hide in the brush. But he ran on, regardless, and as Jeff closed in on him he saw a boy with a rifle ahead. He too was running, towards them, and if the Mexican got the gun—Jeff leaned over in his saddle, swinging his rifle like a saber, and struck him over the head.

He went down in a sprawling heap, and the boy, seeing the disaster, turned back up a trail through the pines. Standifer watched him, scanning the wash below as he brought his charging horse to a halt. Then he rode back and dropped off beside the body of the Mexican, who lay as if he were dead. The sharp edge of the rifle barrel had laid open his scalp, producing a great flow of blood; but his skull, which was hard, was not fractured. Jeff whipped out his handkerchief and bound the wound tight, meanwhile raising the rustler yell for Rover; but as he looked up from his work he saw a Mexican, riding towards him, down the trail which the boy had followed.

With a single, vengeful swoop the Mexican swung down and snatched the rifle away from the boy. Then, dropping behind a pine, he thrust out his gun and fired across the wash at Jeff. It was a challenge, and a summons to the rest of the gang who were lurking back in the woods, and Standifer crouched down behind his man. Caught out in the open, he could seek no other shelter without risking the loss of his prisoner. So he laid his rifle across the prostrate body and drew a bead on the tree.

The Mexican thrust his gun around the side of the tree to shoot, but before he could aim Jeff smashed the bark into his face and drew another bead. Again the rifle crept out, and once more Jeff's bullet threw splinters of bark into his eyes. But as Standifer settled down to smoke him out a big Forty-five slug came at right angles from down the wash and smashed against a rock at his left.

Changing his front Standifer swung his gun to meet it, when the Mexican behind the tree opened up on him. Jeff jumped, for the first bullet had barely missed his head. He was exposed to two fires at once. And as he huddled down behind the body of his prisoner, a copper-jacketed bullet sung past. Another struck a

97

rock with a venomous *spat*—and suddenly Standifer was blind.

Blood and tears intermingled, his ears rang and his head swam. Then as he wiped away the dirt he saw the light again, and felt a sharp stinging in his nose. A flying splinter from the copper jacket of the bullet had grazed the bridge to the bone, cutting a knifeblade gash across his forehead. He could not see his enemies, and as he flattened out to escape their bullets he felt his barricade stir. The sabered Mexican was coming back to life, and as Jeff clutched at him he struck back viciously.

Blinded and exposed to their fire from two sides at once Jeff reached for his pistol and thrust it up against the man's jaw.

"Tell your friends to stop shooting," he cursed. "Or I'll blow the top of your head off!"

For a moment the Mexican resisted. Then he bawled out in Spanish and the storm of bullets ceased. Standifer clung to him, panting, wiping the blood from his eyes while he listened for Rover's shrill whoop. But his enemies were creeping closer and the Mexican with crafty turnings was seeking to elude his grasp. With a last desperate effort Jeff raised his head and repeated the rustler yell; and the answer came, close at hand.

"Whoopee-lah! *Orejanos!*" And the *whang* of Rover's big gun.

CHAPTER XII
Ambush

Many TIMES IN THE cedar brakes of the Guadalupes, when one or the other had tied to a steer—a wild steer that fought the rope and charged to gore his horse—Jeff and Rover had given the rustler yell. It was a yell of savage triumph in the midst of battle, and at the same time a call for help. It announced the capture of another maverick, or *orejano,* and never had they called in vain.

The flow of blinding tears had passed and Standifer could look about him dimly when from the summit of the mesa there came a second shot, and the Mexican behind the tree leaped aside. His body was exposed now to a shot from Jeff and, taking a chance, he whipped up his rifle. The Mexican jumped again—then as Rover opened up on him he leapt up and ran down the trail.

"Here!" threatened Standifer, jabbing his prisoner with his six-shooter, "you hold still, or down comes your meat-house. I've got tired of monkeying with you Mexicans."

They lay quiet, until the stillness was broken by a fusillade from down the wash; and above the rattle of the Mexicans' rifles Jeff could hear a roar that he knew. It was the bark of Rover's big .45-70, and the answers soon died away. Yet, though the battle receded, it sprang up again down the canyon, with one man fighting five. They were in a Mexican country and the odds might soon be greater, but Rover did not return. Still further and further away the old Forty-five barked its challenge and Jeff dug a hole among the rocks. His eyesight had cleared now, though his bloody nose still ached, and he stirred up his prisoner with his gun.

"Get up," he ordered, "and bring me back my horse. And any time you want to make a break, step to it— the bridle is off."

He patted his gun-barrel and the Mexican understood. The time for taking chances had passed. He rose up, staggering weakly as he clasped his swollen head, and obediently he led back the horse.

"Now go over," directed Jeff, "and bring me that other horse." And he pointed to the Mexican's mount, which was standing in the trail by the tree.

For a moment the sullen prisoner regarded him distrustfully, for in Old Mexico it is not uncommon to invoke the *ley fuga,* the law to kill prisoners in flight. But there was no choice but to go, and he brought back the horse, though his eyes often sought the hills. Now that the battle was over, his friends would rally to save him, and it was to thwart them that Jeff caught the horses.

"All right," he said, stepping in between them, "now lead these horses back to your house."

Slowly and reluctantly the Mexican obeyed and, walking between the horses for protection, Jeff followed him, rifle in hand. Over the top of the horses' shoulders he caught glimpses of furtive men, running

100

swiftly to cut them off. Up the steep bank they labored, a horse on each side and the prisoner marching ahead; but as they gained the rim the Mexican horse flew back and jerked his bridle-rein away.

"Ketch that horse, and ketch him quick!" snapped Standifer, jabbing the Mexican in the ribs with his gun; and instinctively he ducked behind his mount. Then it came, the expected bullet, knocking the horn off his saddle while another cut the ground at his feet. He swung around behind his horse, taking shelter against its withers, but he did not lose sight of his prisoner.

"Hurry up!" he ordered; and at sight of his rifle muzzle the slothful Mexican leapt into action.

"You son-of-a-goat," warned Standifer in Spanish, "have a care or I'll send you to hell. Now lead those horses ahead and keep them together—and if one gets away, *adios*."

The Mexican understood, better in Spanish than in English, and his new-found braggadocio disappeared. He hurried ahead across the mesa and, going down the other side, he handled his horses perfectly. Back in the shelter of the houses Standifer looked him over coldly and drew a pair of handcuffs from his pockets.

"Stand up against this post," he ordered; and the Mexican stepped up obediently. The Ranger pulled his wrists behind him and fitted the cuffs closely, leaving him shackled with his arms behind the upright. Then he led the horses inside and sat down. He had caught a bad Mexican, one not unused to deeds of blood if his actions were any criterion, but they were a long way from the Bitterwater jail. A long way from friends and help, and with the brush full of *paisanos* who certainly had learned to shoot.

Never before in the Ranger service had Jeff encountered a band of Mexicans so vindictive and hard to handle, so keen to take advantage and so bold in giving battle, so determined to rescue their chief. And this man whom he had captured, he was no common rustler. There was something behind it all. Somewhere in these peaks there was a prize well worth defending—or they were wanted for other crimes. Standifer confronted him, his hand on his six-shooter, but the bloodshot, angry eyes never quailed.

"What is your name?" he demanded. "And what are you doing here?"

"Ramon Archuleta," responded the Mexican defiantly. "I live here. This is my home."

"And who are these others?" inquired Jeff.

"They are my friends," replied Archuleta. "You will never leave this valley alive."

"Think not?" mocked Standifer. "Well, I'll bet you I do—and take you along with me, to boot. But here comes my pardner, and don't talk back to him—because Rover sure hates a Greaser."

He flung the name at him scornfully and stepped out the door, where Rover was riding up. He was sweaty and bedraggled from riding through the brush and his hands were torn and bleeding; but there was a fire in his eye and when he stepped down, rifle in hand, he scanned the valley behind.

"That's the outfightingest bunch of Mexicans I ever

saw," he panted. "I'm danged near out of cartridges.

Never could git a stand on one long enough to shoot his eye out—what the hell has happened to your nose?"

"Never mind," answered Jeff, "but get your horse inside here before some Mex puts a bullet through him. There's a bunch of them, up on that mesa."

"They're scairt of me," boasted Rover. "I done chased 'em all over the country. W'y, hello!" he exclaimed as he stepped through the doorway, "I thought you killed this rascal!"

He stood glaring at Archuleta, who returned his scowl with interest; then turned and took down his rope.

"Don't you know," he reproached, "that this *hombre* is dangerous? You're making a pet out of a rattlesnake."

He snapped a loop over the Mexican's head and brought it tight with a jerk. "But if you're too tender-hearted," he went on, "I'll attend to him, myself."

"Nope—let him live," replied Standifer. "I need him in my business."

"Now, here!" began Rover, "you may have been a Ranger, but you cain't tell me *nothing* about Mexicans! They're the most treacherous scoundrels in the world, and the thing to do is hang him, right now!"

He yanked the rope roughly and looked up at the rafters, but Jeff laid violent hands on him.

"Come out here," he said, dragging him outside the door, "I tell you I need that man. He's made his brag we'll never leave here alive—and if you hang him we

103

never will. We're surrounded, and these Mexicans are sure *bravo*. They certainly don't act like plain rustlers. They're hiding out for some reason, and just killed that steer for beef. And this man here is their leader."

"That's all the more reason for killing the hound!" raved Rover. "What the devil do you want with him, anyway?"

"In the first place," answered Standifer, "he's my prisoner, and it's our duty to bring him in alive. Didn't we take an oath to support the law! You're a hell of a deputy sheriff!"

"Well, you're a dodrammed fool!" returned Rover vindictively. "Why didn't you shoot him, like I told you to, in the first place? But no, you had to ketch him—and the next thing I knew you had got yourself into an ambush. Look at that hump on your nose, swelled up like a sore thumb! You'll get cross-eyed looking around it."

"Never you mind about my nose," retorted Jeff. "It hasn't affected my brains. This Mex doesn't know it yet, but he's going to get us out of here. And more than that, he's going to go with me and bring in the rest of the gang. I've got it all planned out."

"Well, I'm shore glad to hear it," mocked Rover, bowing low. "You Rangers git awful smart, don't you? But—er—how are you going to persuade him!"

"That's your job," said Standifer. "But don't be too rough with him. Don't fix him so he can't talk."

"I git you!" nodded Rover and stalked inside, just as a bullet struck up the dirt.

CHAPTER XIII
Archuleta Assists

THERE WAS A SMASH of angry bullets against the outside of the log cabin, and threatening shouts from the mesa. The Mexicans had rallied to rescue their chief—but Archuleta was handcuffed inside. Not only was he handcuffed but he was bound fast with Rover's throw-rope, tied in all the fancy knots he could devise; and as the Mexicans grew bolder at nightfall Rover clapped another loop around his neck.

"Tell your *paisano* friends to go on away and leave me sleep," he directed. "Otherwise—" And he hauled on the rope.

The Mexicans left, and in the morning at daylight the edge of the mesa looked bare. But Standifer knew they were lying in wait for him and he turned to his sullen prisoner.

"Archuleta," he said, "I ought to hang you, right now, because I know you'll get me killed if you can. But I'm going to give you one chance. I want those five men who were with you."

"Yes?" returned the Mexican; but as Rover moved towards him the defiant sneer left his face.

"I want them," repeated Jeff, "and I want you to take me to them, and tell them to come in and surrender. They were caught butchering a steer and I want them for rustling. But, by the Lord, if they start to shooting, I'll kill you."

"Very well, sir," replied Archuleta, his cunning eyes glinting. "But first you must untie this rope."

"I'll untie it," blustered Rover, "but I'll put it around your neck and fasten it to the horn of my saddle. So if one of your Greaser friends should happen to knock me off, my horse will drag you to death. And if they *don't* happen to hit me—if they shoot—I'll attend to the dragging, myself."

"Muy bien," shrugged the Mexican. "I am your prisoner. But take these handcuffs from my wrists. I cannot hold the reins, to ride."

"Oh, that's all right," said Rover, "I'll tend to the reins. All you've got to do is holler to your friends and tell them not to shoot."

They lifted their prisoner on to his horse, his hands still fastened behind him, and tied his feet underneath. Then, one on each side, they rode out into the open and Archuleta began to shout.

"Oyez, muchachos! No tiren! Cuidado! Be careful, boys—do not shoot!"

There was a silence, nothing moved; and as Jeff glanced at Archuleta his old, suave smile had returned.

"There is no one," he said, "so do not be alarmed. Now I will lead you to the home of my friends."

"Now look out!" warned Rover, turning to Jeff. "He's just leading you into a trap. That danged old canyon sure looks spooky to me, and he's taking us right down into it."

"Oh, no, my friend," replied Archuleta reassuringly. "Why should I deceive you, now? When you rode in on us yesterday I thought you were cowboys, and with

106

them we have had several fights. But now that I know you are nothing but officers I am satisfied to go to town. I will hire a good lawyer—and how can you prove who it was that killed the steer!"

"Aw, shut up!" came back Rover. "You're one of these talking Mexicans, but I've still got my rope on your neck. So mind your P's and Q's, and the first crooked move you make—"

"Then down comes your meat-house," ended Jeff.

He nodded grimly to Rover, who responded with a wink, and they rode slowly off down the canyon. They were trapped in the enclosed valley, at the mercy of the Mexicans if they chose to put up a fight; but on the day before Rover had chased them several miles—and their leader was now a prisoner. No matter where they were hid they must see the strong rope that was fastened about his neck, and to them its significance would be plain. There had been trouble between the cowboys and the Mexicans of the mountains, and more than one horse-thief had been hung.

So they kept on, confidently; and Archuleta, no less confidently, led the way to a hidden log house. It was tucked away in a narrow canyon, out of sight from the main trail; and as they sighted it Archuleta gave a whoop. But no one answered until, as they approached the loopholed house, Standifer saw a rifle thrust out.

"Look out!" he yelled to Rover and, whipping out his six-shooter, he rammed it under the Mexican's jaw.

"You tell your friends," he barked, "to come out and

surrender or I'll blow the top of your head off. And then, by grab, we'll get them."

"And kill every one of them," added Rover.

He had dropped in behind their hostage, his pistol balanced over his shoulder ready to snap down and shoot at the first move; and Archuleta sat paralyzed between them. It had happened so quickly, this sudden flash of weapons, this swift move to snuff out his life, that his taut nerves had cracked beneath the strain.

"Do not kill me!" he pleaded. "For the love of God, spare me, and I will order my *muchachos* out. Listen, boys," he went on in Spanish, "the Gringos are going to kill me unless you come out and surrender. Do not wait, do not parley, but come out at once. Come out, and lay down your guns."

There was a stir within the house, the sound of a log being thrown away from the door. Then it opened and a Mexican stepped out. He was wounded in the arm, and Standifer recognized him as the man with whom he had had his duel.

"I surrender," he said in Spanish; and laid his rifle and pistol on the ground. Then another and another filed out, until all five had given up their guns.

"Very well," spoke up Jeff, when the last had raised his hands, "if you are peaceful, you will not be hurt. I am a deputy sheriff and I want you for killing that steer."

The Mexicans gazed at him wonderingly, as if doubting their ears; then turned and exchanged significant glances.

"They thought you were cowboys," explained

Archuleta unctuously. But Standifer sensed more than that. For at the words of their leader they only grinned. Something else was in the wind, something the officers did not know about and which the Mexicans would not tell. But with six prisoners on his hands and a long ride ahead of him Jeff had no time to investigate. While Rover took their guns and herded them down to the corral to catch up and saddle their horses, he sat watchfully beside their leader, his pistol poised to shoot, scarcely believing that his long chance had won.

Riding into their stronghold, he and Rover in one day had arrested six Mexican rustlers; and now, with all their guns wrapped tight in a tarpaulin, they were ready to take them to town. On the day before they had fought like devils, but Archuleta had suddenly changed his front. Instead of his old, studied malevolence he was now suavely ingratiating, and he exhorted his men to submit.

"Have no fear," he said in Spanish, "this is the detective from Texas that the great company hired to stop cattle stealing. But how can he prove that any of us killed the steer that was found in the locked-up cabin? I will hire a good lawyer and he will free us at once. Because, of course, we know nothing about the beef. We had just ridden up there when we saw the two cowboys. If I had been guilty would I have stayed there, unarmed?"

"Let him talk," muttered Standifer to Rover. "Our job is to get them back to town. You watch the gang and I'll take the boss. *Andale, hombres—let's go!*"

He led off up the trail, his pistol drawn and ready, never far from Archuleta's back; while in the rear Ralph the Rover herded the gang of Mexicans, who did not conceal their enmity. They were all big, glowering men, quite different from the native *paisanos* who had learned a certain fear of the cowboys. And from their high-peaked sombreros and buckskin shoes it was evident they had come from Old Mexico. Their Spanish was different from the New Mexico brand and they carried themselves swaggeringly in the saddle.

"Wait!" exclaimed a squat, pock-marked *cholo* as they passed the log cabins going back, "I am hungry for some of that beef. We have not had our breakfast, and how can we ride to town with our bellies stuck to our back?"

"Now, look out!" spoke up Rover, "they're up to some deviltry. Maybe they've got some guns hid in that house!"

"Oh, no," explained Archuleta, "my boys are just hungry. Please permit us to cook some meat."

"You stay on your horses," ordered Jeff in Spanish, as he faced the insistent men. "And let me warn you, right now, that my partner hates Mexicans and would love to kill you all."

"But we must have food!" cried the *cholo* with angry vehemence. "And our *compañero* here is sick."

He pointed with his chin at the wounded Mexican, who had his arm in a sling; and Standifer whipped out his pistol.

"Ride out there," he said. "And Rover, tie his hands

to the horn. Who do they think is running this show?"

The Mexican obeyed and Rover tied his hands. Then he bound his feet beneath the horse's belly.

"Now you!" he yapped. And, calling them one by one, he roped them hand and foot to their saddles. At first they protested but at a word from their leader they submitted in sullen silence.

"All right," observed Standifer. "You stay and watch 'em, Rover, while I get a little beef. And if any one makes a break, you kill the whole bunch of 'em. I'm going to get that hide, for evidence."

"That's the talk," applauded Rover. "And I'll do it, for a nickel."

He lolled menacingly in his saddle, one eye on his prisoners, the other on the trail behind, and Standifer strode down to the cabin. The door still hung open, where Rover had broken it down, and the half-butchered beef lay on the floor. But as he turned it over, to cut out the brand, a big square of hide was gone. Some Mexican, during the night or in their absence down the canyon, had removed the marks of ownership—for the ears had been slashed away, too. Jeff glanced out the door to where the prisoners were watching him and it seemed, to his jaundiced eyes, that Archuleta was smiling. But Standifer did not hesitate. Working carefully and methodically, as if the brand was still there, he cut out a section of hide and wrapped it up in a bundle. Then, carving out a chunk of beef, he returned and tied them on his saddle.

"We'll be going on," he announced, "and stop and cook this later. I saw a man, just now, up on the mesa."

He fell in behind Archuleta and, with his pistol ready to shoot, motioned him grimly on towards the pass. The Mexican glanced at him cunningly but at the prod of the gun he led the way up the trail. Again he looked back, but Jeff's face did not change, though his last legal evidence was gone. He had arrested the rustlers and, case or no case, he was going to take them to jail.

CHAPTER XIV
A Husband's Honor

THEY TOPPED THE pass in safety and dipped down the other side, towards the plains and distant Bitterwater. But as they halted to cook some beef Standifer saw a band of horsemen, riding rapidly in from the south.

"Them's Mexicans," announced Rover, reaching back for his rifle; and, raising his sights, he placed three bullets so close that the leaders came to a halt.

"I knowed it," he said, "they've come to take our prisoners. That's the bunch from this Mexican town, Pilon."

"They'll never get them," stated Jeff, kicking dirt over the fire and swinging up on his horse. "And the first man that tries to stop me will go home in a blanket. These Mexicans have been badly spoiled."

"Not by me," asserted Rover, taking a shot from the saddle. "I know how to handle them, to perfection. And don't ride too fast—they might think we were scairt of them. I'm shore glad we're out of that brush."

They had come down out of the pines and the cedar-covered ridges to the wide, rolling prairie below; and while their pursuers, well out of range, hung close on their flank they headed across the plains on the trot. The wounded Mexican groaned and begged them to stop, making extravagant gestures towards his arm, and Archuleta tried to protest; but Standifer drove him on until, far across the flats, they could see the silvery river, and Bitterwater.

The day was near its close and the Mexicans, tied to the saddle, made much of their aches and pains. Jeff himself felt a weariness which he would not admit and the cut across his forehead throbbed and stung. But, riding wild behind him, Ralph the Rover was in his glory, emptying his rifle at the scurrying Mexicans. They had increased in numbers until now over a hundred followed after them towards the town, for the year before a band of cowboys had invaded Pilon and more than one native had been killed. Two Texans had met their death and the feeling was so high that a race war might easily spring up. Yet, though they followed so menacingly, the Mexicans did not shoot and Rover gave up in disgust.

"The danged yaller-bellies," he cursed as he fell in behind his prisoners. "One Texan could lick a thousand of them. Look at that dust, down on the flats! That's the boys, coming from Bitterwater. But we don't need no help—do we, Jeff?"

Standifer grunted and shifted his weight in the saddle as he watched the flying cowboys approach.

Some were rustlers themselves, some little men opposed to the Company, some Mill Iron hands under Jack Flagg; but Rover's round of shots had brought them all and as they whirled past they gave the high yell. They rode circles around the prisoners, looking them over with baleful glances, exchanging coarse pleasantries with Rover; then with a rush they were gone after the Mexicans of Pilon, who had dared to threaten a Texan.

Jeff rode in slowly, escorted by the cowboys who had turned back not to miss any fun; and as he passed the hotel he spied Annabelle on the gallery, looking down with startled eyes. He saw her again as a mob surged out and stopped them, in front of the Bucket of Blood. Then as he stepped down from his horse she came running to meet him, and his heart gave a jump and stopped. He had left town without seeing her, without even a word after his days of unexplained absence; and now, unshaved and bloody, his head in a filthy rag, he stood staring, for there were tears in her eyes.

"Oh, Jeff!" she cried, throwing her arms around his neck and kissing his grimy cheek. "Are you hurt? What's the matter with your head?"

"Nothing at all, Pet," he answered, as the crowd turned to watch them; and he blushed deep, under his tan. This was not the reception he had expected from Annabelle, but he tried to act his part.

"Did they shoot you?" she demanded eagerly, gazing up at his bloody face. "Come in and let me take care of you."

"Just a scratch," he said, "from the jacket of a bullet. I've got to put these prisoners in jail, and then I'll be down to see you."

"Please come!" she whispered, leaning closer; and he nodded as he turned away. Many eyes were fixed upon him as if trying to read his heart, to pry into the secret between them; but he rode away soberly, leaving Rover to do the talking.

When he had come back before he had avoided this woman whom he had acknowledged before the world as his wife. He had ridden away without even a word of greeting—and yet she had welcomed him home. In spite of all the gossip which his actions must have caused she had rushed through the crowd to kiss him. But did she love him, or was she acting a part? What-ever the answer his duty was plain and he rode straight back to the hotel.

Annabelle was out waiting for him, looking very sweet and winsome, and his heart smote him as she held out her hands.

"Come up to my room," she said, "and let me bathe your head. I want to talk with you—Jeff."

"Yes—Annabelle," he answered; and again the blush mounted until his wind-burned cheeks were aflame.

"I'm sorry," he began, as they mounted the winding stairs; and her hand crept into his.

"Never mind," she responded. "I'm so glad you're back again! What brutal-looking ruffians they were!"

"Oh, the Mexicans!" he replied. "Yes, they put up quite a fight."

"And did they really try to kill you?"

"I'll bet you!" he exclaimed. "And if it hadn't been for Rover I might have cashed in my checks. This cut over my eyes made me blind."

She opened her door and for the first time, reluctantly, he entered Annabelle's room. Then she closed it and confronted him reproachfully.

"Yes, I know," he said. "I had no business to neglect you and I'm awfully sorry, Annabelle. Did it make things worse, for you?"

"Yes, it did," she admitted. "And I hated you for it, Jeff. But when you didn't come back, and I heard about your quarrel with Jack—I was afraid I'd lost you, then. People said you had skipped out of town. The women all thought we had quarreled and separated, and I was so mad I let them believe it. But when I saw you, all bloody, and with those terrible-looking Mexicans, I forgot all about it, Jeff. Can you forgive me for kissing you that way?"

She gazed up at him archly and Standifer scratched his head.

"I believe I can," he said, "if you'll promise not to do it again. Certainly is mighty embarrassing to a man of my shrinking nature to receive such attentions in public. And a danged sight worse to have these people think I'd quit a nice girl like you—they believing, of course, you're my wife."

"Oh, Jeff," she murmured, stepping closer, "sometimes I almost think I am. We quarrel so, you know."

"That's right," he sighed. "But this time I was wrong, and I'm game to admit it, Annabelle. Now go ahead and take off that rag."

He submitted his head to her tender ministrations and as she bathed his throbbing wounds and tied a bandage around them her hands seemed more than kind.

"There," she said at last as with a final pat she stood off to admire her handiwork, "that's the first thing I ever did for you. Now sit down and tell me about the fight."

"I would," he smiled, "only I want to hear about you. And then I'll have to go and get shaved. Have you been up to call on your stepmother?"

"No, I haven't!" she declared. "Because I know if I do she'll step in and take charge of my life."

"How do you mean?" inquired Standifer curiously.

"Well, you see," explained Annabelle, "when Father married again I couldn't get along with my stepmother. She was only a few years older than I was, and the giddiest little thing you ever saw, and yet she tried to rule me like a child. It was simply ridiculous, and Father sided with her in everything so—well, that's when I commenced going with Jack. Of course I'm glad I didn't, now, but I was going to marry him, just to have my own way, for once. We had agreed to run away—I was awfully foolish, then—but would you believe it, she was listening and heard our plans, and reported me to my Father!"

"I see," nodded Jeff. "Well, what then?"

"Why, Father was simply furious, because he knew Jack was a drinking man—he's terrible when he's drunk. So he bundled me off to a girls' school near

117

New York and I stayed there until I was eighteen. I was mad, at first, and I never did like it there; but when it came time to go home I knew I had never loved Jack. He was just the first man I'd ever seen and—but you know all about that. So now here I am, shut up in this hotel with nothing to do but dawdle around, and I can't even go to see Father. Because, of course, he'll ask questions—and how can I answer them? But I did send up for my horse."

She paused significantly and Jeff glanced at her sharply.

"Did you go for a ride?" he asked.

"Yes," she answered, "and of course Jack followed me. It wasn't my fault, Jeff."

"Well, who said it was?" he demanded. "I suppose he went along with you?"

"Why, yes," she responded innocently, "only—"

"I'm going to tell that whelp," he burst out savagely, "to leave my wife alone!"

"But I'm not your wife," protested Annabelle.

"It makes no difference—people all think you are And I know what Jack Flagg is up to. He's trying to get back at me for hitting him over the head!"

"Why, Jeff!" she exclaimed mischievously. "I believe you're actually jealous. But Jack and I have always been friends."

"Well, why don't you marry him, then, if you think so much of him? Don't let me stand in your way!"

He was trembling with rage and for the first time since she had known him his anger was directed at her. But Annabelle had a temper of her own.

"Because I don't want to!" she retorted. "But is that any reason why you should forbid me to even talk with him?"

"I've got a reason," he said. "A good and sufficient reason. You're supposed to be my wife. And as long as you are I'm going to protect your honor—and my own!"

"Oh," she mocked. "*Your* honor!"

"Yes, mine," he repeated. "My honor as a gentleman—and as a fighting man, to boot. I can see right now that Jack Flagg will never be satisfied until he looks down the muzzle of my six-shooter. But until that time comes you remember what I've said. I'm here to protect you—as my wife. But of course," he went on, "if you want to tell the truth—"

"Oh, no, Jeff," she pleaded, "I couldn't! Can't you see it would ruin my life? I didn't think, when I went with Jack. But if you'll only be patient and put up with me, Jeff!"

She laid hold of his coat and drew him closer, then slipped her arms about his neck. "Please, dear!" she entreated and as she clung to him beseechingly the anger in his eyes died away.

"I'll do anything for you, Annabelle," he said at last, putting her hands aside. "Only remember what I say. A wife is as much obligated to protect the honor of her husband—"

He stopped, for Annabelle had bowed her proud head and buried it against his breast.

"Yes, yes—I'll remember," she sobbed. "And oh, Jeff—"

119

She paused, gazing up at him through tear-dimmed eyes; and suddenly she kissed him, passionately. Then she turned and fled and Standifer awoke, groping his way down the winding stairs.

CHAPTER XV
Incomunicado

A COLD WIND buffeting his cheek as he stepped out the door, brought Standifer back to earth. He had moved in a sort of dream since, for no reason that he knew of, Annabelle had kissed him again. Kissed him passionately and contritely and fled from his presence like a child who has admitted a fault. It was not like Annabelle, at all.

Her father had told him—and he had learned it for himself—that she was willful and hard to control. She had ways of her own for accomplishing her purpose without seeming to oppose him at all, but kisses and tears had not been among her wiles when she had persuaded him to pose as her husband. He had yielded then without knowing that he yielded, out of a distorted sense of chivalry. But now *she* had yielded, and kissed the hand that ruled her, when at last he had asserted his will. She had promised to remember his words.

It was not much that he had asked of her—no more than any husband should expect from a dutiful wife—but Annabelle was not his wife. He wondered wearily why she clung to the pretense when all the town could see it was false. Was it to escape from her step-mother—to stave off Jack Flagg when he came to remind her of her promise—or did she do it for love of him? That was a thought that called for the drinks.

He felt weak and unstrung and as he passed the Bucket of Blood he turned towards the swinging doors. But as he started to enter he was halted in his tracks by the big, booming voice of Rover. He was telling the story of their fight. Jeff drew back and peeped in through the crack of the door, curious to hear the lurid account, for Rover was never trammeled by facts. But as he ran on now in his grand, triumphant battle-chant Jeff could hear another voice, breaking in.

"Like hell you did!" it scoffed and the crowd began to laugh; but Rover kept doggedly on.

"How many did you kill?" cried the high, derisive voice; and Jeff swung the door to look in. Rover was sitting in state on the high, mahogany bar with a crowd of laughing cowboys gathered about; and in the midst of them, head and shoulders above the rest, rose the tall, hulking form of Jack Flagg.

"Didn't count 'em," answered Rover. "Too danged busy dodging bullets. Did you see that scar on Jeff's nose? He got grazed by a slug, and another one cut his forehead. Made him blind—he couldn't see, or he'd've killed the last one of them. The blood ran into his eyes."

"Where does he bury his dead?" inquired a deeper voice; and Jeff saw the smirking countenance of Flagg. He and his gang were heckling Rover.

121

"Never mind!" flared back Rover. "It's shore lucky for you he was trained in the Texas Rangers. They make it a rule to give every tough the first shot or he'd've killed you long ago. Yes sir, they killed so many men the people protested—seemed like it was done in cold blood—so Captain Ross gave an order never to fire the first shot. Give the sons-of-goats a chance."

"Who do you mean by sons-of-goats?" demanded Jack Flagg truculently. And Rover stuck his chin out at him, sneering.

"Well, you're blatting the loudest!" he answered. "And don't you never think I'm skeered of you. You'd better draw in your horns or I'll knock 'em off, and put a ring in your nose."

"You're drunker than I thought you were," retorted Flagg, laughing hectoringly; and the crowd took up the shout. Jeff closed the door softly and went on up the street—Ralph the Rover could take care of himself. But this talk of Flagg's was a studied attempt to influence public opinion against him. In spite of Jeff's warning Flagg had gone his way—riding openly with Annabelle, sneering covertly at his courage, boldly daring him to take offense. He was hunting for trouble, but Jeff could not meet him now. He had other duties to perform.

The town was full of people, for court was in session; and, milling around the jail, a crowd of curious cowboys were waiting to catch a glimpse of the prisoners. They turned to stare frankly at the new deputy sheriff who had arrested the gang of Mexicans, and for the first time since his arrival Jeff was aware of a grudging approval in the eyes of the men he passed.

There was a feud of long standing between the Texas cattlemen and the earlier Mexican settlers, a feud which had accentuated their natural race antipathy until a word could bring on a war. When the Mexicans had controlled the county they had punished with great severity the law-breakers from this alien race, and when at last the Americans gained control they had dealt fully as harshly with the Mexicans. And, where the early Texans had refused to submit to arrest at the hands of Mexican deputies; it had now become almost as difficult to bring in Mexican prisoners, especially from the mountains to the east.

There the Mexicans of Pilon and the neighboring sheep and cattle towns had boldly defied arrest; and Ralph the Rover's tale of the battle among the peaks had stirred up the war-spirit anew. Even the rustlers and their sympathizers, who had eyed Jeff askance, were moved to a certain admiration; for in making his arrests he had shown a nice discrimination which had allayed the worst of their fears. He had come among them boisterously, clubbing Jack Flagg over the head the minute he stepped off the train; but he had only arrested a Mormon butcher and the six Mexicans he had just brought in. Six Mexicans so *bravo* that the crowd had rushed to see them, only to be turned back at the door.

"Mr. Standifer," hinted the sheriff as Jeff entered the office, "there's a great deal of interest in those prisoners you brought in. And so far nobody in town can identify them. Don't you think it's a good plan to kinder let the boys file in and look at them in their cells?"

"No, I don't," answered Standifer. "I want them kept strictly *incomunicado*. They're a bad bunch of *hombres* and if you let people come in they can demand to see their own folks. They've got something they're concealing from us, and they're crazy to pass the word out—maybe to bring in the gang and stage a jail-break. I don't want them to have a lawyer, or nothing."

"Well, that's their right," stated Smith Crowder as with a disgruntled limp he turned back and slumped down in his chair. "And another thing, Standifer, you ain't in Texas now. I'm the sheriff, and these people are my constituents."

He jerked his thumb towards the door where the disappointed crowd was voicing its discontent, but Standifer only shrugged.

"Can't help it," he said. "If I'd've exercised my full rights I could have killed that man Archuleta. I took this bloody nose, and a big chance to boot, to bring them back and convict them. And that's what I'm going to do."

"Well—how?" demanded Crowder, sulkily.

"By keeping them *incomunicado* until they spill what they know. Has the district attorney been in yet?"

"No. He's busy. There's his office."

The sheriff was angry now, and perhaps a trifle jealous of this new deputy who was stealing his laurels; for except for some town arrests Smith Crowder had done very little in upholding the majesty of the law. His short leg and corpulent body made riding a great hardship—and the rustlers, one and all, had votes.

But Eugene Sutton, the district attorney, was a different type of vote-getter. For him there was only one record that counted. and that was of criminals convicted. He was a small man but aggressive, with the tense, nervous watchfulness of a terrier, and he made the new deputy welcome.

"Just a minute," he said, "until I sign these papers. You're the very man I was looking for."

He dashed off his signature and beckoned Standifer into a private room where they could talk without being disturbed.

"Mr. Standifer," he began, "I'm glad you came back in time to be a witness against Ike Cutbrush. The Grand Jury has handed down an indictment against him, and I honestly believe we'll convict. I decided, as a matter of policy, not to press the cases against his sons. He's a Mormon, as you know, and until you brought in these Mexicans it looked like religious persecution. But the Church of Latter-day Saints is opposed to rustling, on principle, and I've decided upon a rather bold stroke. I hope you'll approve of it, Jeff."

He leaned back, smiling, and Standifer watched him curiously. It seemed to him he was a little complacent.

"As you know," he went on, "it has been practically impossible to get a conviction in this county for rustling. But I feel confident I can convict Ike Cutbrush. I'm going to challenge every man for this jury unless he's a Mormon, in good standing. That will give the Mormon people a chance to go on record. There will be no way to dodge the issue. The evidence is conclusive. They are trying one of their own erring brethren. The verdict, I feel sure, will be: Guilty!"

Standifer stared, a little resentfully, as Sutton crossed his legs and demanded his opinion of the move; but his poker face did not change. The idea, of course, was his own, passed on, perhaps, by Captain Bayless—but all that he wanted was a conviction.

"Why, yes," he said, after a judicious pause, "that looks like a very good plan. Have you seen these six Mexicans I brought in?"

"Well, no," admitted Sutton. "I hope you've got as good a case against them."

"No case at all," confessed Jeff. "And they don't act like rustlers, either. I'm satisfied, from watching them, that they are Old Mexico Mexicans, and I believe they're up to something. Their leader, Archuleta, although he can't read or write English, seems to know quite a little about law; and what I want to do is to keep some shyster lawyer from turning him out on bail. They've got something they're concealing—something big!"

"Well, just what evidence have you?" inquired Sutton cautiously. "I've heard that they're desperate-looking men."

"The first thing against them is this nose," grinned Standifer. "I got that in a regular gun-battle. Now men wouldn't fight and resist arrest like that unless there was something behind it. My idea is they've got some

126

plunder, hidden out in those hills, because here's the way it all happened."

He ran briefly through the story of the conflict and Sutton nodded, approvingly.

"You're right, Jeff," he said, "and I'll tell you what I'll do. I'll request the judge to fix a high bail, and we'll keep the Grand Jury in session until the last thing before court adjourns. Because if we go before it now, with nothing but this piece of hide, we can hardly expect an indictment."

"Good enough," agreed Standifer. "And don't you tell anybody that the brand is cut out of that hide. I don't believe even the Mexicans have caught on to my bluff—that's another reason for keeping them close."

They shook hands on the bargain, for their interests were identical; and, waking or sleeping, Jeff never left the jail long enough for a messenger to slip through. Mysterious Mexicans began to drift into town and gravitate towards the county jail; but Standifer was watching and, at the end of four days, Archuleta gave over his demands. At first he had asked for lawyers, for a conference with his friends, for the privilege of communicating with his family. He had blustered and threatened but Jeff was adamant and Rover patrolled the jail-yard at night. But on the fourth day he asked humbly if he might send out his laundry and Standifer granted his request.

Each day a comely Mexican woman had appeared at the door with food and tobacco for the prisoners, but as she stood waiting eagerly for the bundle of soiled clothes Jeff held up a detaining hand.

"Un momento!" he said; and spreading the clothes on his table he looked them over carefully. Against the light the stinking shirts revealed nothing; but as he examined the seams the stained fold of an undershirt caught his eye. He turned it back and under the lap he made out three words, in Spanish: *Muevele los caballos.*

"Move the horses!" Why had he never guessed it before? The valley among the peaks was a rendezvous for horse-thieves. And in the confusion of their arrest the guilty Mexicans had had no chance to move their *caballada.*

"Here are your shirts," he said to the staring woman, bundling them hastily into her arms. But as she gathered them up he pulled out the telltale undershirt and hid it under his coat. That night with a posse of cowboys he headed out across the plains, riding hard for the Spanish Peaks.

CHAPTER XVI
King Cole

TWO DAYS PASSED, while the Mill Iron cowboys raked the ridges back of Spanish Peaks, and then at dawn they came pounding into Bitterwater with twenty-two stolen horses. They had been hidden up a blind canyon, not quarter of a mile from the cabin where the band of Mexicans had surrendered, and four of them had the Mill Iron on their hips. Four of the best—and one black, King Cole, was the top horse of Jack Flagg's string.

Jeff eyed him admiringly as they dashed in across the flats on the last lap of their triumphant return. He was a high-headed horse, glossy black except for his stockinged front feet; and when he ran he held his tail up like a banner, while his mane flowed out like a cloud. A snorty horse, full of life and virile power. But of course he belonged to Flagg's mount.

They poured pell-mell into the big Company corral that adjoined the Headquarters Building, and from their beds under a wagon-shed the home cowboys roused up and welcomed them with a yell.

"There's my Rowdy hawse!" whooped a Texan. "Been looking for him everywhere. Hey, Jack—there's Topsy and King Cole!"

Flagg sat up, heavy-eyed from his evening potations, and ran his eyes over the horses. Then he turned to the gate, where Jeff Standifer was watching him, and gave an ungracious grunt.

"To hell with him!" he grumbled. "He's a bunch-quitter, anyhow. He knowed when the round-up was about to commence and pulled out to duck the work."

"I'll take him!" offered the Texan cheerfully; but the range boss cut him short.

"No you won't," he said. "I'll ride him myself—with the spurs."

King Cole circled the corral and snorted rebelliously as he heard the voice of his master. Then he turned and circled again and as he went by the gate Jeff pushed it a little ajar. There was a shout as he plunged towards it—a rope whistled after him—but King Cole had sighted freedom and he smashed against the gate, only to halt as a loop encircled his neck. Jeff had let him out and then roped him on the fly, and now he brought him back.

"Here's your horse," he said, offering the rope-end to Flagg; and the range boss glared at him malevolently.

"Keep the knot-headed old plug!" he cursed. "Do you think I'd take him from you?"

Jeff pulled King Cole up to him and, rubbing his nose, slipped the noose off over his head.

"That's a good horse," he said admiringly; and turned him loose with a sigh. But Captain Bayless had stepped in, and overheard him. Following the habits of a lifetime he had got up at daylight, just in time to see the horse-herd pass by.

"He's yours, then," beamed the Captain. "You've earned him, Jeff. And boys, here's something for you."

He stood smiling in the gateway, and as the cowboys grinned expectantly he fetched a bottle out from under his coat.

"I just thought," he suggested, "you might like a little drink. Yes, I mean it, Jeff—the horse is yours."

"Mighty kind of you," responded Standifer as he passed the bottle on. "But Mr. Flagg has got the first claim, I reckon."

"No, I hain't!" bawled back Flagg. "I wouldn't have the black brute. You been fishing for him—now keep him and be damned to you!"

"Now, Jack!" reproved Bayless, "remember who you're talking to. And remember who the horse belongs to. He's a Company horse and since Mistuh Standifer brought him back—"

"Well, *take* him! Who wants him?" yelled Flagg, stamping his boots on; and he ran out to intercept the bottle.

"Very well, Jeff," smiled the Captain, "the horse is yours, as a mark of appreciation for your services. Ike Cutbrush has been convicted!"

"Good!" pronounced Jeff. "I'll just take the King along with me."

He built a loop and stepped out towards King Cole, who was watching him with wary eyes; and the cowboys, too, paused to look. If he missed his throw, their jeering laughter would mock him; but he dragged his loop carelessly in the dirt. The black stepped to one side, his feet set for a rush; but when Jeff lifted his rope, King Cole stopped. He turned as quickly the other way, but the man was before him again; and once more the rope came up. Twice more the big horse started, but the dread of the dragging rope each time checked his headlong rush. He stood still, snorting softly, and without a word Jeff flipped the loop over his head.

"You're my horse now, Coley," he said; and King Cole followed obediently after him.

"You're quite a horseman, Jeff," observed Bayless as they passed out into the street. "Quite a horseman—and quite an officer, if I'm any judge. Seven rustlers, inside of a month."

"Pretty good," admitted Standifer, "but Mormons and Mexicans don't count. You wait till I tackle the Texicans."

"Now, Jeff," coaxed the Captain as they went past his door, "you come in, and let's have a drink. Because that's just what I want to talk about."

He led the way into his office and after a drink of the best they sat down by the newly-lit fire.

"Seven men, seven rustlers," repeated Bayless. "And these Mexicans are a desperate crew. "There's no doubt in the world that every one will be convicted. But what about the Texans? That's the question! And yet I'll never be satisfied until Bill Longyear is behind the bars. He's the leader of these rustlers, and very insolent in his behavior. I've heard him declare openly that the Company steals a hundred where he and his friends steal one."

"Yes," assented Jeff, "we've got to get Longyear if we ever expect to stop rustling. But it's going to be hard to convict him. They'll soak a poor Mormon, or a bunch of Mexican horse-thieves, with all the pleasure in life; but the first time I lay my hand on a Texan the fireworks are going to begin."

"You anticipate a fight, do you, Jeff?"

"Yes—shooting," agreed Standifer. "You can't get around it. Although so far I've done pretty well. But when I get my man in jail—that's when the battle starts. You can't get a jury to convict."

"Well, why not?" demanded the Captain at last.

"For the same reason," answered Jeff, "that Bill Longyear gave. Because the people really believe that the Company does more stealing than all the little men combined."

"But we don't!" declared the Captain defiantly.

"Maybe not," shrugged Standifer, "but *somebody* is stealing. I know that for a certainty. I never saw so many hair-branded yearlings in my life as there are running loose on this range. And when you find hair-branding there are only two explanations. Either the Company's own men are standing in with the rustlers, or they're making a lot of mavericks for themselves."

"Oh, now Jeff!" protested Bayless, "please don't try to poison my mind against Jack Flagg. This hair-branding and all the rest of it was done last year, when old John Dobbins was range-boss. Jack has promised to straighten it out and the round-up will begin just as soon as we get good grass. I'm sorry you two can't get along together, but don't oppose him, Jeff. And come around and see me oftener."

"Every time I come around here," returned Standifer bitterly, "I have another run-in with Flagg. That's why I stay away. And when the round-up begins and I go out to watch the branding—then hell is going to pop. But remember, I'm not hunting for trouble. I'm sorry, in a way, that you gave me that horse, because of course it will stir up bad blood. But I'm glad, in another way that I got Coley away from him. I hate to see a man abuse a horse."

"Well, Jack is a little rough, when he's been drinking," admitted the Captain. "In fact, that's one reason I gave you King Cole. He's a great favorite of Annabelle's, and I was very glad indeed to see how gently you handled him. You're a strange man, Jeff—you're so gentle with horses and so rough with men."

"That's my business," said Jeff, "to be rough. It's the

only way the job can be done. And the first time I weaken or take water my value as a Ranger ceases."

"I can see that," nodded Bayless, "because I've been a Ranger, myself. But don't be too rough, Jeff. Now that you've got those seven rustlers take a few days off, until the big round-up begins. Be friendly and sociable with the boys that are working for me. Didn't you find your posse all fine men? Well, unbend a little and become your true self and you'll win a legion of friends."

"Nope," decided Standifer. "What's the use of pretending? They know what I'm here for and what I think about this stealing. I think it's done by some of the Company's own men. And I don't want to make friends with a man, and then turn around and arrest him."

"But within reason, Jeff!" coaxed the Captain. "At least you can be friends with me. And come around some evening and call on Mrs. Bayless. She would be very glad to receive you."

"Thank you, Captain," replied Jeff, without committing himself. "It's very kind of you both, I'm sure."

"Jeff, do me a favor," began Bayless at last. "You have heard about our Cowboys' Ball. We give it every year, before the round-up begins, and the people come for miles. It's a great social event and all our neighbors are invited, no matter who they are. We bury the hatchet—even the rustlers are welcome. For one night we are all just neighbors and friends. Won't you come to the ball—and bring Annabelle?"

"Why, yes," responded Standifer; and then he

stopped short. "No, hold on," he cried, "there's something behind all this. That was a long preamble, Captain, just to bid me and Annabelle to the ball."

"Well, I'll lay all my cards on the table," laughed Bayless. "For years it has been the custom for Annabelle to lead the dance and be Queen of the Cowboys' Ball. The boys want her to lead it again."

"Lead it with whom?" demanded Standifer, his eyes suddenly narrowing; and the General Manager came out with it.

"With Jack," he said. "Jack Flagg. He's King of the Cowboys that night."

"Then he can dance with somebody else," declared Jeff, rising up. "Do you think I'd let him dance with Annabelle?"

"Well, why not?" challenged Captain Bayless; and suddenly his voice was stern.

"Never mind," answered Standifer. "She'll never dance with Jack Flagg. Not as long as she's my wife."

"Very well," returned the Captain, after a long, hard look at him. And Jeff turned and clumped out the door.

CHAPTER XVII
For the Company

A WEEK PASSED, and with magical quickness winter was gone and summer had come—summer with grass underfoot and the cottonwoods full-leaved and cowboys dashing to and fro. In the Company corral the big wagon was run out and the chuck-box put in behind. Then the bed-wagon was overhauled and stored with horseshoes and branding-irons and coils of new, grass rope. The cook set up his fire-irons and got out his dutch-ovens to feed the cowboys who came swarming in. Winter had gone and summer had come and the Cowboys' Ball was due, but it was still winter in Jeff Standifer's heart.

Something had come between him and the woman he called his wife, though there were those who scoffed at their marriage. He had gone to see Annabelle, mounted gallantly on King Cole, but she had declined to go out for a ride. Then, to get out of town, he had rounded up Rover and all that week they had been riding the range. The cattle were shedding now, losing their long, winter hair and revealing every mark and scar, and hair-branded yearlings were every-where.

On some the bars had been left off of the Mill Iron, and already Bill Longyear with brazen effrontery had been burning the circles into a Hog Eye. ⊖ Other rustlers, equally enterprising, had beat the round-up to it and started a big Frying-pan brand. o– But the brand which puzzled them most was a new one on the range. A Pig Pen # —two lines crossed like the rails of a pen—and no one claimed the iron. It was not registered in the Brand-book and yet not ten miles from Bitterwater there were calves that carried the brand. Big calves that had been sleepered, or hair-branded on the range so that only the bars remained. To Jeff and Rover, trained to read every brand— equally trained to detect every burn—it was as plain as handwriting on a wall. The Mill Iron cowboys had turned against the Company. They were banded together in their stealing. But who were the owners of this new, Pig Pen iron, which had been burned over so many Company brands? Even Rover, in spite of his association with the rustlers, professed to be at a loss. No one claimed them—but they showed up everywhere.

When the round-up began and the thousands of scattered cattle were thrown together in one big, bellowing herd; then, unless all signs failed, there would be Pig Pens by the hundred and Captain Bayless would know he had been robbed. He was a cowman of the old school, as quick as any other man to recognize a brand that had been altered. But would he then at last admit the guilt of his own cowboys, men hired and retained by Jack Flagg? Would he fire them, as he had threatened, and bring in Texas gunmen to defend his rights on the range? Or would he play along with his range boss? Either way, there was sure to be war—unless he got rid of Jeff.

A hatred had grown up between the two men, an instinctive and deep-seated antipathy. Everything that Jack did seemed wrong to Standifer and Flagg hated the ground that Jeff walked on. They were like flint and steel—when they met the sparks flew. And neither would draw back or quit. When Jeff had learned that the fine horse he now rode belonged to his rival's string, King Cole did not look any the less good. He looked better—he loved him—and something within him began to scheme and plan to possess him. It was not by accident that Jeff had stood at the gate when the stolen Mill Iron horses had been brought back. Nor was it unpremeditated when he elbowed it open and roped Coley as he charged for freedom. Some devil of enmity had put the thoughts into his head, and Captain Bayless had done the rest. He had given Jeff his range boss's top horse!

Standifer rode into Bitterwater the morning before the dance, sitting proudly on his prancing black steed. King Cole was high-spirited and the touch of a spur would make him caracol and dance, but Annabelle did not look out. At the Bucket of Blood, Rover reined in precipitately, leaving Jeff to follow if he would. But it was no time for him to indulge in a drink—he was due to call on Annabelle.

Never before in their brief acquaintance had she refused his slightest wish or shown the least desire to oppose him. But on his last visit Annabelle had changed. Perhaps she had heard of his ultimatum to her father, for she was miffed, and received him coldly. When he had invited her to ride she had pleaded a headache and complained of the wind and sand. And so Standifer had learned that all dreams must end and that even his goddess was human. Somebody—perhaps her father—had repeated his statement that he would not let her dance with Jack. Or perhaps she was still seeing Flagg!

It was that thought which had driven Jeff out of town, to rake the range for more proof of Jack's guilt; but as he rode back to the courthouse, and his bare room in the jail, he decided to make amends. After all she was only a woman, living shut up in a gloomy hotel and deprived of all the pleasures she loved. He would take her to the dance, to the Cowboys' Ball, and let her make her peace with her parents. He would dance with her himself and permit her to dance with others. Only she could not be the Queen with King Jack.

There was a crowd by the jail door as Standifer rode up—a crowd of Mexicans, standing sullen and expectant—and at sight of them his heart suddenly sank. Had the horse-thieves been acquitted? Were their friends waiting to see them discharged? But as he fought his way in he found Smith Crowder snapping on the handcuffs. The Mexicans had been convicted and were about to start to prison.

They stood silent and resentful, their black eyes smouldering as two deputies shoved them about; but at sight of Standifer a greater hate overmastered them and they spat out Mexican curses.

"Here, Standifer!" called out the sheriff, "you're just in time to help take these prisoners to the train. They drew five years in Yuma and they're acting kinder snakey. All right, Ike—we'll take you, too."

He swung open a clanging door and Ike Cutbrush stepped forth, holding his hands out for the cuffs.

"Oh, that's all right," said Crowder. "I won't shackle you, like a Mexican. You walk along with me."

He led the way out and the long procession started—more rustlers than had been convicted in many a year—but Standifer followed in the rear. It was no pleasure to him to see these seven men consigned to the hell-hole at Yuma, nor did he wish to appear as the man who had captured them and gathered the evidence to convict. They plodded over across the track to the little wooden station where a crowd was beginning to collect, and as they waited apathetically for the train to come in the saloons gave up their men.

The town was full of cowboys—and rustlers, too—gathered fraternally for the Cowboys' Ball. Too fraternally, Jeff thought, for a loyal Company man had no business resorting with cow-thieves. But the more he rode the range the more it was borne in upon him that the Company men and rustlers were one. They were working together, some hair-branding, some rangeriding, some running off stolen stock. They came over together now, shouting jocular warning to their friends to mend their ways; and with them, tall and laughing, came Jack Flagg, the range boss, King of the Cowboys for that day.

Head and shoulders above the crowd, he was their natural leader, and as Cutbrush saw him laughing, he scowled.

"Yes, laugh!" he cursed. "They'll be gitting you next. You dodrammed, widow-robbing Texican!"

"Aw, that's all right, Ike," responded Flagg good-naturedly. But Cutbrush was not to be quieted.

"I may have stole a beef," he yapped. "But you're the biggest cow-thief of all. Only, of course, *you* steal for the Company. I'm jest a pore, Mormon butcher."

He glanced malevolently in the direction of Captain Bayless, who started and turned pale with rage.

"Never mind," jeered Flagg. "Your own brethren convicted you, so I reckon you're good and guilty. Say, send me a hair-bridle, Ike."

"I'll send you a bullet, when I git out!" threatened Cutbrush. "You're the man that put me where I am. You and them Mill Iron cow-punchers that come down through our valley and run off even our milk-cows. You drove me to it—you and old Captain Bayless—only of course *you* were stealing for the Company."

He put such a wealth of implication into his words that Bayless blenched, then strode over to the sheriff.

"Smith," he said, "tell your prisoner to keep still. And why haven't you got him handcuffed?"

"Oh, he's all right," grinned Crowder, "only he's talking too much. Shut up, Ike—here comes the train."

He looked up the track, where the local had come in sight, but Ike did not shut up.

"I'm telling you!" he shouted defiantly. "They'll be gitting you next, Jack Flagg. You done played out yore string and that smart detective is onto you. I'll be looking fur you, down at Yuma."

There was a silence then, broken only by a rumble as the train came down the grade, and Flagg glanced about uneasily.

"Aw, shut up!" he said at last.

"I won't do it!" shrilled Cutbrush. "They'd've got you, long ago. Only of course, *you're* stealing for the *Company!*"

He stabbed an accusing finger toward his sulky

enemy, but this time his taunt brought an answer.

"No he ain't!" yelled a voice from the crowd. "He's stealing for himself. I know him!"

Every head turned at once and there, smiling blandly, stood Ralph the Rover, drunk already.

"He's stealing for himself, Ike, and we'll send him along, right soon. Don't you worry—you won't be lonely."

The thunder of the train drowned out Ike's surly response and the curse that came from Jack Flagg, but as it pulled out of the station with its prisoners safely aboard Captain Bayless seized Jeff by the shoulder.

"Fire that man," he raved, "or I'll fire him for you." But Standifer only shrugged.

"Fire us both, and be done with it," he answered. "Do you think I can swing this alone?"

"Well—keep him, then!" snapped the Captain, turning red with suppressed rage. "I said I'd keep my hands off—and he's drunk."

"Drunk or sober," repeated Jeff, "he's the only friend I've got here. And I reckon I'm going to need one.

CHAPTER XVIII
The Queen Decides

THERE WAS FIRE in Standifer's eye as, ignoring the staring cowboys, he went to pay his duty-call on Annabelle. The scene at the station, the parading of handcuffed rustlers before the cowboys who had come to the ball, had not added to the *entente cordiale.* On this day of days, when the hatchet was supposed to be buried, Smith Crowder had summoned a ghost to the banquet. Not one man out of a hundred on the crowded streets of Bitterwater was guiltless of rustling in some form, and their enmity centered on Jeff.

He it was who had arrested Cutbrush and run down the gang of Mexicans who had been started on their way to prison. And to their jaundiced eyes he was a Nemesis with a six-shooter, a man who would get them next. Though he did not return their stare they felt his keen glance, and they knew he was ready to shoot. So they watched him in somber silence as he passed down the street and entered the Hotel Bitterwater.

Annabelle had not been feeling well—or so Mrs. Collingwood reported—and when she came down there was a suggestion of resentment in her eyes, which before had always been smiling. Or perhaps her smile had died at sight of his stern face, still set from running the gauntlet of the rustlers. She glanced hesitantly at Mother Collingwood then, almost with a sigh, led the way into the parlor and shut the door.

"Oh, dear," she said, "I don't know what's the matter with me. I don't think I'll go to the ball."

"Suits me," nodded Jeff. "I'd be just about as welcome as a striped skunk at a camp-meeting."

"But they've all asked me to come," went on Annabelle, changing her mind. "So maybe we'd better go."

"All right," agreed Standifer. "I'll call for you this

evening and put up the best front I can. But this town is so full of rustlers you can't get on the sidewalk—and Smith Crowder just took seven to Yuma. That's a nice, cheerful send-off for the Cowboys' Ball, but the old boy has got to make a show. He paraded them out in handcuffs and Ike Cutbrush was so mad—"

"Oh, don't talk about it!" cried Annabelle, shuddering. "Have you seen Father since you came back? He's so anxious to show we're reconciled! And my dearly beloved stepmother has been very nice, for her. So of course we'll have to go. I just hate it, in one way; and in another way—well, I'll certainly be glad to see the boys. You know, when I was little, the cowboys kind of adopted me—it was so funny to hear them all stop swearing. And every year, at the Cowboys' Ball, they always insisted that I should lead the first dance. They called me the Queen, and all that."

She glanced up at him artlessly, and Jeff saw where the conversation was leading; but he did not try to divert it. She wanted to be the Queen of the Ball, but she knew what he had said to her father. And now, of course, she was trying to win him over. But did she really want to dance with Jack Flagg?

"You'd make a great Queen," he said, impersonally. "I suppose you've got your dress made, and everything."

"Well—yes; I have," she admitted. "Won't you let me be the Queen—this once?"

She laid her hand on his shoulder and gazed up at him beseechingly—and then she drew her hand away. His eyes had answered for him.

"I told your father," he stated, "what I don't doubt he told you, that I didn't want you to dance with Jack Flagg. Is he going to be King, tonight?"

"Why, yes. He's the range boss, you know."

"And do you want to dance with him, Annabelle?"

She hesitated, for his voice had almost deceived her, it was so gentle and guilelessly mild; but she remembered, and shook her head. She knew how he hated Jack.

"No-o," she said. "But I *would* like to be the Queen, Jeff—and receive my loyal subjects, and all that. It's been the custom for years, and now that I've come back—"

"Why, certainly," he said. "You can be Queen."

"And can I dance with Jack?" she cried before she thought; then set her teeth in her lip.

"Why, certainly," he said again, so unbelievably kind that she gazed into his eyes, bewildered.

"Why, what do you mean, Jeff?" she asked.

"I mean," he said, "that I want you to be happy—as happy as you can be, Annabelle. And if you want to dance with Flagg I won't stand in your way. It will be a good time to end this foolishness."

"Why, Jeff!" she exclaimed, taken aback. "You don't mean—"

"Yes, I do," he burst out vehemently. "I'm tired of all this pretending. I'm tiring of posing as your husband. But as long as I do pass for the man that you're married to I'll never let you dance with Jack Flagg. I don't want you to see him, or talk to him, at all—and you know the reason why."

145

"Well!" cried Annabelle, stepping back and tossing her head; and suddenly she was laughing recklessly. "Thank the Lord," she said, "I'm not really married to you. And if that is your idea of how a husband should act I'll just naturally *go*—and lead the dance."

"Suit yourself," answered Jeff. "I don't want to boss you. But on the day that you forget your obligations as my wife, and your duty to protect my honor, I will report to your father just exactly where we stand and take the first train to Texas."

"All right!" she flared back, accepting his challenge. "I might as well be dead as denied all pleasure and shut up in my room like a nun. You can do whatever you please. Because I'm most certainly going to that dance!"

"I'll take you," responded Standifer. "And you can do what you please. But, thank God, we're only making a bluff at being married, and I'll be damned glad to have it over with."

He grabbed his hat and whipped out the door, too angry to see where he went; but as evening came on and the festivities began he remembered his promise to Annabelle. This was the closing night of the little drama they were acting, a play which had cost him many a heartache, but was none the less dear for that. And now that it was ending he resolved to carry it off as gallantly as a gentleman should.

From the iron-bound trunk which held all his belongings he brought out a suit made by an expensive tailor, a silk shirt and a gorgeous puff tie. He polished up his best boots and after a visit to the barber he dressed himself in his best. But as he was starting for the hotel he took out one of his pistols and tucked it under his waist-band, far back. The best hack from the O.K. Livery Stable bore him down to bring the Queen, and when he stepped through the door Jeff's heart was almost light, though he wondered what Annabelle would say.

They had quarrelled when they parted; but as she came down to meet him, daintily supporting her long train, she smiled upon him radiantly.

"Why, Jeff!" she cried, surveying his clothes in mock surprise. "I declare, you look almost like a gentleman."

"I used to be one," he bantered, "before I quit the Rangers and hired out as a roughneck detective."

"Well, why don't you quit again, if you don't like it?" she jested.

"If you knew how hard I've tried," he answered grimly, "you wouldn't say a word. That old man of yours won't turn me loose. I've been downright insulting—called him everything but a horse-thief. But ump-mm—he needs me in his business."

"Have you really tried to quit?" she asked reproachfully as she settled down in the hack beside him. "That wasn't very complimentary—to me."

"No, it wasn't," he admitted. "And I acknowledge the fault. But there's some kind of a Jonah been on me in this town and I'll be right glad to get out alive."

"Don't you know, Jeff," she said, laying her white hand on his arm, "when I saw you tonight it brought it all back again—that time I first saw you, on the train.

Only you haven't got the wolf skin coat."

"And the cady hat!" he added, laughing. "Old Rover attended to that."

"He isn't such a bad man, is he?" she said. "Only it seems as if he's always drunk."

"They all are," he stated, bluntly. "Worst drinking town I've ever seen."

"But you don't drink—do you, Jeff?"

"Well, not so you'd notice it," he answered. "I woudn't last a week, if I did."

She paused and glanced up at him curiously.

"Are you always going to be a detective?" she asked.

"I don't know," he responded. "It's a good deal like drinking. Sort of a habit, and you can't get over it. And every time I quit some old rascal like your father wires in and hollers for help. There's no use telling them that there are a thousand other men willing and anxious to take the job. No use telling them you don't want it and won't take it. They'll go behind your back and get your old Ranger captain to practically order you out."

"You never told me that before," she murmured. "I thought you liked it, Jeff."

"Well, so-so," he admitted. "When I'm into it. But I'm in pretty deep, tonight."

He nodded his head towards the unfriendly crowd that was gathered about the Company House and Annabelle laughed again, softly.

"I'll protect you," she promised. "Didn't I do it once before, out in front of the Bucket of Blood?"

"You sure did!" he responded gallantly as he leapt

148

out of the hack and offered the Queen his arm. And, smiling up into his eyes for all the world like a doting wife, Annabelle tripped lightly into the ballroom, while the company stared in amazement. On the reliable testimony of Mother Collingwood and her chambermaid they had quarreled not three hours before. There had been high words and threats, and the name of Jack Flagg had been bandied to and fro; but now they entered as joyously as any newly-weds, every glance a lover's caress.

Mrs. Bayless hurried to meet them, her hands outstretched, a small, pretty woman but with too sweet a smile to make Standifer believe all she said. He bowed low as he took her hand and murmured his thanks as she bade him make himself quite at home; but he could see that she was watching him, for the gossip from the hotel had swept over the town like a grass fire. And if Annabelle, in her long gown of pale blue silk, with ropes of pearls about her neck, appeared a little haughty and remote, it was no more than could be expected of a queen.

The headquarters building had been cleared for the affair, and the three great rooms joined by sliding doors. In the first one the round-up cook and several assistants were busy with their barbecued beef. The second was the reception and retiring room. The third had been furnished with benches along the walls and a dais where the musicians stamped and scraped: and there, at the entrance, Captain Bayless welcomed the men while their ladies retired within.

"Ah, Jeff, my boy," he beamed, shaking hands with

him most cordially, "we are certainly glad to have you come tonight, and bring Annabelle to be our Queen. Doesn't she look rather regal for just a little girl that has been allowed to run wild over the plains? But nowhere in the world, suh, will you find a greater chivalry than right here among our cowboys."

"She certainly looks the part," nodded Standifer. "How's the Cowboy King carrying his liquor?"

A shade of anxiety passed over the Captain's face as he glanced about the room.

"The boys haven't come yet," he said at last. "But now, Jeff—no trouble tonight!"

"Not of my making," promised Standifer. "No matter what happens. I've told Annabelle she can do as she pleases."

"Well, that's certainly very generous of you!" exclaimed Bayless, much relieved. "And now, if you'll excuse me, I think I'll summon the gentlemen. The Grand March will begin, very soon."

He bustled out the door to send messengers through the town to bring in his tardy cowboys, and Jeff sat down on a bench. Along the wall in stiff groups sat the settlers' wives and daughters, all dressed in their Sunday best, while here and there some diffident swain was negotiating for a dance. There would be no wallflowers at the Cowboys' Ball—they outnumbered the girls, two to one—but the bright lights of the saloon had drawn the men like moths, and wives and sweethearts were left to themselves.

There was a whoop down the street, the festive *whang* of some cowboy's six-shooter as he took a shot at the moon; and then, bronzed and rugged, they came trooping in and made a belated rush for their partners. The bashful ranch-girls who had sat so long unattended were suddenly besieged with suitors; and as the fiddlers, again and again, played a bar or two of music, the excitement knew no bounds. They lined up in a straggling row behind the Captain and Mrs. Bayless, waiting impatiently for the King and Queen. But Jack Flagg and the Wild Bunch who ran with him had lingered for a final drink.

From the door of the waiting-room Annabelle stepped out hesitantly, a crown of cottonwood leaves, eternal emblems of spring, gracefully entwined in her wealth of black hair. For a moment her eyes swept the room, as if seeking the Cowboy King; but when they fell on Jeff, standing close beside her, she smiled and took his arm. All eyes were upon them as they stood side by side, the tall, grim-faced cowboy and the girl who, rumor said, had married him to spite Jack Flagg.

The minutes passed, and scurrying cowboys went out to search the streets; and still, serenely, she chatted on with her husband, ignoring the buzz of gossip. Mrs. Bayless fluttered her fan, though the room was not warm, and the Captain tugged angrily at his goatee. After all his machinations to have Annabelle the Queen, the King of the Cowboys had gone back on him. He was carousing, perhaps, in some saloon down the street, oblivious of his duty to the lady. Or perhaps out of pure deviltry, to pay back her slight, he left Annabelle a kingless Queen. But at last, with a rush they came.

In the lead, a wreath of flaunting cottonwood leaves about the crown of his big, white hat, Jack Flagg strode regally in; while behind him the Wild Bunch, his faithful satellites, stamped and rollicked as they followed their chief. For that day and every day, he was indeed the Cowboys' King; for his word was law on the range. And now he came on confidently, seeking the hand of the Queen to open the Cowboys' Ball.

She was standing with Jeff, and if she saw the King enter she did not meet his eye. Only the crowd, drawing away to make room for him, gave evidence of Flagg's approach. In his red shirt and dove-colored trousers, his high boots and leaf-crowned sombrero he looked every inch a king, and as he shouldered his way through the cowboys he looked around with a reckless grin. Never glancing at Standifer, who had stepped to one side, he doffed his broad hat with a flourish and made a low bow to Annabelle.

"May I have the honor of your company," he asked, "to open the Cowboys' Ball?" And the wide hall was suddenly still.

No one there but had heard of Annabelle's quarrel, and the stern ultimatum of her husband. Yet Jeff, standing up very straight, only drew a deep breath, and sighed. If there rushed through his brain the thought that this was the end, that his dream was over forever, he gave no outward sign; and Annabelle, pale and silent, gazed from him to Flagg as if seeking to make up her mind. The Cowboy King waited—still smiling, still confident—and at last the Queen made reply.

"I am sorry," she said, "but my husband does not approve. So I shall have to decline the honor."

"You what?" demanded Flagg, after a moment of stunned silence. And Annabelle stripped the crown from her head.

"I will not be the Queen," she declared.

He glanced about uncertainly until his questing eye found a girl who answered with a smile.

"All right," he said and, snatching the wreath from his hat, he jammed it down over her hair. "Let 'er go, boys!" he called, waving his hand at the orchestra. And so the Grand March began.

They paced by, couple by couple, as Jeff stood aloof, his fierce eyes fixed straight ahead; but as the music changed abruptly to a waltz he felt a hand on his arm.

"Shall we dance, Jeff?" asked Annabelle, demurely; and he awoke as if from a trance.

"Yes, Annabelle," he answered. And when their eyes met she smiled up at him, worshipfully.

CHAPTER XIX
A Right Pretty Widow

WITH ANNABELLE IN his arms, and every eye upon them, Standifer danced on in a daze, hardly conscious of the glare which he received from Jack Flagg as they passed. He was showing his liquor now, where a minute before he had seemed to be perfectly sober; but Jeff knew how the blow of Annabelle's refusal must have made the range boss reel. It had staggered *him,* though it had made him very happy.

He had dreamed, no denying it, dreamed as lovers have always dreamt—and then he had seen the dream fade. Jack Flagg had come between them with his broad, reckless smile, his swaggering, masterful ways. But Annabelle had made her choice. Even when they had been riding to the ball she had not been unmindful of her problem—asking him questions, trying him out. And then she had given Jack his answer.

But now not a word passed between them about that quarrel, so much better forgotten. Annabelle was gay and smiling, there was a spring to her step as they circled on to the lilting waltz, and Jeff fell into the spirit of her mood. His step was as light, his smile as joyous, and when it ended her hand clung to his.

"Let's sit this one out," she said as he escorted her to the long bench. "If my admirers will give me a chance!"

They converged upon her, smiling doubtfully, asking the pleasure of a dance; but she had one answer for them all.

"No, boys," she said, "I don't see much of Jeff. So we'll dance while we've got the chance."

"Might as well," agreed Standifer, "because the round-up begins tomorrow, and Rover and I will be riding."

"Then let's dance!" cried Annabelle, jumping up and taking his arm. "Why didn't you tell me you could dance?"

"I never got a chance," he grinned. "And say,

Annabelle, *you* can dance."

"I'm so happy, I could fly!" she confided in his ear. "But, Jeff, be careful with Jack. I could smell the whisky on his breath."

"You promised to protect me," he jested. But she drooped her eyelashes warningly.

"Not from Jack," she answered. "He'll be ugly, after this. Just look at him carrying on."

After leading the first dance, to save his face, Flagg had dropped out, taking the Wild Bunch with him. He stood at their head now as they gathered close together, watching the dancers as they came whirling past; and their loud and boisterous talk showed their mood. They were planning to break up the dance.

"Let's sit this out," pleaded Annabelle as the music suddenly stopped; and they sought the far corner of the room. "I'm afraid," she whispered; but Jeff laughed.

"Well, I'm not," he said, "so that's all right. He hasn't got the nerve to tackle me."

"He'll kill you," she shuddered. "I know it."

"No, he won't," replied Standifer. "He's afraid to shoot it out with me. I've given him two chances, already. It's those side-kickers of his that I'm scared of."

He scanned the hard faces of the little knot of cowboys who gathered about the tall figure of their chief, stamping each dissolute visage on his memory. "That little guy is the bad one," he added.

"But Jeff," she reasoned, "don't you think it would be better if we went, before something happens? I can explain it all to Father, afterwards."

"No, Annabelle," he answered smiling. "We might as well have a good time together, before hell in general breaks loose. And if this gang of toughs down me—which of course they may do before I get through with my job—you'll sure make a mighty pretty widow. Prettiest widow I've ever seen."

He glanced down at her admiringly and Annabelle blushed, though her hands were working nervously.

"It doesn't seem right to speak so," she said, "but— do you really think I'm pretty?"

"That's a kind of leading question," he responded gallantly, "and of course I was just talking about widows. But in case something unfortunate and unforeseen should take place I'll admit that you're pretty, right now. And just to show these old hens that we've made up our spat, let's dance as long as we can."

He rose up and bowed and she surrendered to him, smiling, letting her eyes dwell only on his; and so until midnight, while the company stared, they paced the witching measure of the dance. It was like a solemn requiem over the ghost of their vanishing happiness; a farewell to the joy which could endure but a single evening and then, mothlike, must die—and as they danced the Wild Bunch watched them. King and courtiers alike had given over the pretense of worshipping at another throne. The newly-crowned Queen was cast aside, and Jack Flagg had taken command. They had set out to break up the dance.

The musicians had struck up a schottische and,

while Jeff and Annabelle sought a seat, the tireless dancers charged lightly down the room.

"They're stampeding, boys!" yelled Flagg in mock alarm. "Throw 'em over! Put 'em into a mill!"

With a great clatter of boots, like the gallop of flying horses, the Wild Bunch circled the hall. They pressed closer, turning the dancers nearer and nearer to the center until they stopped, tied up in a mill. So on many a dark night they had turned the leaders in a wild stampede, pushing them over to the left until they were milling round and round and their rush was halted for good. It was a joke, but Annabelle was alarmed.

"Now let's go home," she pleaded, smiling wanly. "I'm so happy—but I'm tired, too."

"I'll order the hack," offered Jeff, solicitously; but as he stepped out into the light and gazed down the street he saw two men, half in the shadows. A tall man and a short one—very tall and very short. It was Jack Flagg and Shorty Updegraf, and as he appeared he saw them look back. They had slipped out of the hall after breaking up the dance, and Standifer knew they were watching for him. But he did not mention it to Annabelle.

She came out, attended by her father and step-mother, who wished her an affectionate good-night. Nothing was said of the denouement of their care-fully-laid plan to have her lead the ball with Jack Flagg, but as Standifer shook hands with Mrs. Bayless he could see that she was eaten with curiosity. They had heard so many things, and really knew so little,

157

about Annabelle and her Ranger husband; and now, after all the stories of their quarrels, they found them as gentle as doves.

Jeff helped his wife into the hack with the grace of a courtier and Annabelle glanced up at him, smiling; but after they had escaped the keen scrutiny of her stepmother she gave way to her former fears.

"Draw the blind down, Jeff," she whispered. "They might see you, and follow us. Oh, I just hate a man that drinks!"

"Don't worry about *him*," soothed Standifer as he hastily lowered the curtain. "A drunken man isn't often very dangerous. They can't shoot straight enough, for one thing."

"But Jack can," she insisted. "And I could see he was angry when you and I began to dance. Wasn't that girl that he danced with terrible?"

"I didn't notice her," confessed Jeff. "Some rancher's daughter, I reckon."

"No, she's a—she lives down at the dance-hall, Jeff."

"What?" he cried. "Did he pick her out on purpose, to put a slight on you?"

"Oh, no, no!" she protested. Don't be so suspicious, Jeff. He just took the first one he found. But I saw the other women all looking at her so strangely, and my stepmother told me who she was."

"Well, never mind," he sighed as they drew up at the hotel door, "the whole town is crazy, anyway. And we certainly gave the ladies something to talk about. That'll hold 'em, while I'm gone."

"Where are you going?" she asked as they stepped inside; and impulsively she drew him into the parlor. "I want to talk to you," she said, very low. "Come in— and shut the door."

Jeff followed into the warm and stuffy room which was as near as they came to having a home. It was there that they met, and generally quarrelled. But the greatest quarrel of all was over. She would never flirt with Jack Flagg again.

"I wanted to tell you," she began, "how sorry I am that I started all this trouble with Jack. And now please, Jeff, keep away from the round-up. If you go, I don't know *what* will happen!"

"Neither do I," returned Standifer. "But if I *don't* go, Annabelle—"

"Oh, I know—they'll think you're afraid! But please be careful, and don't talk so rough to them. Do you want me to be a widow, Jeff? You know you said I'd make a right pretty one!"

"Well, you would," he acknowledged gravely. "But sometimes I think—I believe I can fool 'em, yet. But I've got to play my cards my own way. So you run on to bed and let me fight this out and perhaps—"

He drew her swiftly to him and kissed her trembling lips. "Perhaps I'll come back," he said.

CHAPTER XX
The Big He-Wolf

WITH HER KISS still on his lips and his brain in a whirl Jeff fled from the presence of Annabelle; but as he slammed the hotel door and headed up the street he remembered Jack Flagg and drew back. They would be waiting for him, somewhere—and Shorty Updegraf had nerve. Standifer reached for the six-shooter tucked far back under his waistband, and brought it around to the front. Then he stood in the shadow of the doorway and listened to the sounds of the night.

The roulette-wheel in the Bucket of Blood was chattering merrily, he could hear the deep notes of the big double-bass as the Cowboys' Ball went on; but no high-heeled cowboys came clumping down the boardwalk to demand redress, and revenge. Yet Flagg had seen him pass. He drew back closer and with Indian patience stood silent in the deepest shadows. The street was empty now, but sooner or later they would show themselves.

Inside the hotel he heard light footsteps departing and Annabelle's door closed softly. What impulse had swept over him, while they were talking in the parlor, to make him steal a kiss? For certainly Annabelle had not led him on—they were talking about her being a widow. And, for all the world knew, if he were way-laid that night, she would be just that—his widow.

Perhaps some premonition had put the words in his mouth and prompted him to steal one kiss. Perhaps they would get him that night!

He moved uneasily and peered in through the door.

The dimly-lighted lobby was vacant—and there was a door that led out behind. With a last glance down the street, which was too empty to suit him, he slipped quietly in and out again into the alley, which was as empty as the street in front. From the backdoor of the Bucket of Blood there came a rumble of drunken talk and the clatter of hurrying feet. Then a man ducked out and took refuge behind a barrel, piled high with empty bottles. It was Updegraf, the cowboy with nerve.

From the first time he laid eyes on him Jeff had recognized in the sawed-off Shorty a man who would shoot—a gun-fighter. He was small, but his eyes were resolute; and his high cheek-bones spoke of courage. In the shadow of the back steps Standifer watched for his next move, and then a second man approached. Big and dominant Jack Flagg strode out into moonlight, his hand hooked into his gun-belt; and instantly Jeff started towards him, as if just coming out from the hotel.

Flagg halted, and took shelter behind a shed; but when he recognized his enemy he stepped out again and confronted him.

"You lying whelp!" he burst out angrily. "I've got the dead wood on you at last! You're no more married than I am. I've been watching you, damn your heart, and you've never spent a night in that hotel!"

"Well, what is it to you?" demanded Standifer. And Flagg choked as he mouthed a great oath.

"I'll show you what it is to me," he cursed. "I was engaged to marry Annabelle, the day she stepped off that train, and you stole her, you cheap, smart Aleck detective!"

"You hair-branding cow-thief!" retorted Jeff. "Don't you think you can run a blazer over me. I've seen *hombres* like you before, but I've never met one yet that would draw his gun—and shoot!"

He stood poised, his hand on his pistol, and Jack Flagg was taken aback, for he had not known Jeff was armed. But a stir behind suddenly reminded him of Updegraf and he stepped out of the line of fire.

"Yes, and you can tell that little shrimp," went on Jeff, "that you hired to do your shooting, to come out from behind that barrel. Otherwise there's liable to be a hog-killing in this town. Come out of there, Shorty—I'm on to you!"

He whipped out his pistol and the little man, like a jumping-jack, popped up with his hands held high.

"Don't shoot!" he quavered. "You've got me!"

"You bet your boots I've got you," answered Jeff. "And I've got your big, fat friend. Now unbuckle your gunbelt, and step away from it, quick. Come up here—I want to see you!"

The gunman obeyed while Jack Flagg in sullen silence stood idly on one side. He had been out-guessed and out-bluffed and the killing spirit had died in him at the first flash of Standifer's gun-barrel. It covered them both now and Shorty advanced quickly, sticking his hands up again from habit. For a second Jeff scanned his battle-scarred countenance, noting the fear in his guilty eyes; then he spoke again to him, sharply.

"You get out of town before daylight," he ordered. "I'm the old he-wolf in this town."

"Yes, sir," responded the cowboy, scuttling off; and Jeff turned to face Jack Flagg.

"All right, Mr. Flagg," he said. "I'm not scared of you a damned bit. You attend to your own business, and I'll attend to mine, and we'll see who comes out on top. But next time you come after me—come a-shooting."

"I'll do that," promised Flagg, starting off. And Standifer let him go.

There was a weakness about the range boss that Jeff had not counted on, for he was a big man and reputed to be a brave one. But now once more he had refused to draw and shoot, and behind such rank cowardice there dwelt treachery. The town was full of cowboys who had the nerve he lacked and who, at a hint from the Cowboy King, would hide in dark alleys to waylay him. Even Shorty might turn back to do his boss's bidding, and Standifer returned to the jail. But when daylight came he crossed the track again and searched the saloons for his enemies.

Drunken men lay everywhere, on the floors and in the alleys, but no one looked up as he passed. Even the barkeepers were overcome by the liquor they had absorbed—it was like a city of the living dead. He was searching the hay in the O.K. Corral when he came upon Rover, paralyzed. On that day of days when he needed him most Ralph the Rover would be sleeping it off.

Jeff looked at him again and saddled up King Cole, who snorted and stared fearfully about. There had been wild doings that night and the drunks had frightened him—the round-up would not begin with the dawn. In the Company corral the cowboys lay sleeping, encased like mummies in their tarps; but as he circled the yard, still on the lookout for Shorty Updegraf, Standifer saw a tousled head rise up. It was Jack Flagg, sleeping it off, and when he saw Jeff he grunted and covered up his face. There was no fight in him now, nor in any of the Wild Bunch, and Jeff rode back to the jail again, satisfied.

Stretching out on his cot he slept like the dead until the sun was two hours high; and then, at a shout and clatter, he roused up to see the round-up start. First the cook in his rumbling wagon, with the pots and pans jangling, went rattling down the street, whooping raucously and popping his whip. The bed-wagon followed, while drunken cowboys, reeling and clutching, rode pitching horses hither and yon. All was noise and confusion, with men falling off and others, though never so drunk, sticking on; and then with a rush of hoofs, the *remuda* went flying past, the horse-wrangler hot on their tails.

Last of all came Jack Flagg, after a conference with Captain Bayless. Sitting his mount like a centaur, searching the saloons as he passed for signs of his errant hands, he rode out at the head of his men to start the first circle of the day. Already the wagons had trundled off across the prairie to the cutting-ground behind the first buttes. There was order, after all, in the chaos. And now with his cowboys behind him, he rode forth to rake the range. He was the king of all that country, once he got clear of town, but as he left he glanced about furtively. There was one man he still looked for—Standifer.

But the Ranger who had shamed him and driven his gunman out of town was lying low, for once. He looked on from afar, and Annabelle, from the gallery, became the object of Flagg's pent-up wrath. She had stepped out to watch them pass, vaguely fearful of some great catastrophe hanging over the man she loved. All her high hopes had departed with the night which had given them birth and she had awakened repentant and afraid. Jack met her anxious eyes and turned away sullenly, then he glanced up and eyed her again.

"Hello, Annabelle," he shouted brazenly. "Where's Good Eye, this morning? Out hiding behind a blade of grass?"

He threw back his head in a mighty roar of laughter and his drunken partisans joined in, to a man. But Annabelle, sensing the hate behind their raucous laughter, stepped inside and closed the door. The cowboys, fifty strong, rode orgulously on their way as if challenging the lone Ranger to show himself. Before they had been divided, scattered hither and yon in line-camps; but now they were united in a solid, fighting front, ready to assert their full mastery of the range.

They gathered outside of town and the range boss, dividing his men, sent them trotting off across the plain. Half swung to the east, dropping man after man behind as the leaders pressed ahead on their circle; and the other half rode down the river. By noon they would have gathered the scattered cattle along the flats and pushed them on to the cutting-ground; and then, changing horses and snatching a bite at the chuckwagon, the cutting and branding would begin. Every calf as he was roped would be followed by his mother, and no man who had ridden the range like Standifer could doubt what the outcome would be. There would be Mill Iron cows lowing over hair-branded calves, and calves turned into the Hog Eye and Frying Pan. And, mixed with the rest, a big bunch of yearlings that had been altered into the mysterious Pig Pen.

Jeff loitered about the corral, saddled and unsaddled King Cole, waiting in vain for Ralph the Rover to sober up. The last of the cowboys had recovered enough to ride, but Rover remained dead to the world. He had been drugged, to deprive Standifer of his assistance in a fight; and to ride out alone was to court death. But to stay away was to admit defeat. From the window of his room Jeff had heard Jack Flagg's taunt and the laughter of his loud-mouthed cowboys. Would he stay hid, behind a blade of grass?

With two pistols in his gun-belt and his rifle beneath his knee, and mounted on snorty King Cole, he rode out of town alone; but at the crossing he was aware of a horseman spurring after him and Captain Bayless came splashing across the ford. He sat very straight on his highbred bay, the picture of a warrior with his white moustaches and fierce goatee; but he carried neither pistol nor gun. To him the good old days of the six-shooter were gone and he glanced at Jeff's guns disapprovingly.

"Where are you going?" he inquired. "To the roundup?"

"Why, yes," admitted Standifer. "Thought they might be expecting me and—"

"Aren't you afraid," demanded the Captain, "after what passed last night, that you might have some trouble with Jack?"

"Afraid?" repeated Jeff; and then he laughed. "Why, no," he said, "no trouble at all! I'm just going out to look the cattle over and see how the brands tally up."

"Yes, but suppose Jack should resent your overseeing the branding! It has been definitely agreed between us that Jack shall handle the cattle while I attend to the office-work. He's always been rather touchy about his rights."

"I imagine he has," responded Jeff, dryly. "But, Captain, you're a cowman—or used to be—and you know as well as I do that calves have been sleepered, and so on."

"Now, Jeff!" expostulated Bayless, "I can see you have let your prejudices carry you farther than I would go with Jack. In fact, I think that Flagg has behaved very admirably, not to take more serious offense. So if you don't mind I'd like to ride along with you—and I've left word for Smith Crowder to come out. He'll be back on the Ten Forty-five."

"The more the merrier," quoth Standifer. "But maybe it would suit you better if I didn't go out there at all? All you have to do, Captain, is say the word."

"No, no!" protested Bayless, hastily. "I don't mean to reflect on your courage—or to imply that I don't need you, Jeff. I just came in the interest of peace."

"All right," grumbled Standifer, "if that's what you're looking for. I thought we had a war on our hands. I got held up last night by a couple of your cowboys and had to run one bad-man out of town."

"Why! Who was that?" cried the Captain.

"Never mind," returned Standifer, "you'll probably miss him, sooner or later. Unless he happens to show up at the round-up."

He grinned sardonically and Bayless stroked his long goatee as he turned and looked back towards town.

"I wish Smith Crowder would hurry up," he said. "He has a wonderful influence over the cowboys."

"Here too!" agreed Jeff. "And I'd feel a lot safer if I had old Rover along with me. But somebody doped his whisky—leastwise, he's still down and out—so I'll have to play my hand out, alone."

"And what do you anticipate?" inquired Bayless. "A fight?"

"Well, a run-in, anyway," admitted Standifer. "It's my job to look over those brands. But of course, if you still think that Jack Flagg is honest, and a loyal employee of the Company—"

"I do, indeed!" declared the Captain warmly. "And I

168

don't want any trouble between you. So I'll supervise the branding myself, Jeff."

"Good enough," agreed Standifer. "And if Smith Crowder comes out—well, you might say, you don't need me, at all."

"Oh, yes I do!" exclaimed Bayless, suddenly panic-stricken. "I can't get along without you. But just for today, Jeff, while they're recovering from their drinking—"

"Take the play," waved Jeff, and rode on his way laughing. The war had been taken from his hands.

CHAPTER XXI
The Round-Up

On THIS FIRST DAY the show-down would come, when rustlers and Company men would line up against the Ranger who had been brought in to break up their stealing. Jeff knew it and the rustlers knew it, for they were there at the wagon when he rode up in company with the Manager. The cowboys, out on the circle, saw his black horse from afar and knew that their challenge had been answered. Good Eye Standifer had not hidden behind a blade of grass—he was there, to look over the brands. Only Bayless, the General Manager, closed his eyes.

At the chuck-wagon the cook had dug a long hole and burned a pile of cedar to coals. Big oil-cans full of beans and stewing dried fruit were suspended from the pothooks, ovens of beef were on the coals; and on the cover of his chuck-box Uncle Joe, the harried cook, was mixing biscuits with lightning speed. He glanced up briefly as his new guests approached, returning the boss's 'Good morning'; but for Jeff he had not even a surly nod, and the rustlers regarded him as dourly.

Bill Longyear was at their head, with two pistols in his belt and his running-iron stuck under his saddle-flap; and forty men sat their horses behind him. As cattle-owners and stray-men they had a right to be present and eat at the Company wagon, but, now that the Cowboys' Ball was over, Captain Bayless cast all pretense aside. Here were the very men who were battening off the Company, building up their little herds from his calves and the *orejanos* that they caught on his range. Yes, men who had made mavericks by butchering the cows, while they branded the orphaned calves. He looked them over with a grievous smile and retired to the top of the butte.

"Did you see that man, Longyear?" he demanded of Jeff as they dismounted beneath a lone cedar. "See that running-iron, and the telescope behind? He actually glories in his stealing and dares me to catch him—you get his hide and I'll give you a thousand dollars!"

"Don't need it," jested Standifer. "It's sure fine to be alive and just laze around in the sunshine. And there comes Smith Crowder, riding along out of town. Why don't you give the money to him?"

"Jeff," reproved the Captain, "this is no laughing matter. This rustling has got to be stopped. And it never will be stopped until Bill Longyear and his part-

170

ners are put behind the bars."

"Well, no use to arrest them," observed Standifer philosophically. "The jury will just turn 'em loose. So I'm going to stretch out and take a little snooze—this is one day I don't have to work."

He sprawled out luxuriously in the half-shade of the cedar tree and put his hat over his eyes, but as a clatter of hoofs announced Smith Crowder's approach he sat up and looked around. The great circle had grown smaller—the cattle were coming close, led in by the wise old cows. Every year, and twice a year, they had seen the cowboys coming; and they had learned the one way to escape. So, sedately, lowing and mooing, they fell into the old trails which led to the hard-stamped cutting-ground, and the calves and young stuff followed. Soon the roping and branding would begin, when the young calves would first feel the iron.

"Well, well!" exclaimed Crowder as, pounding heavily up the hill, he reined in his winded horse. "What's the hurry, Captain Bayless—what's the hurry!"

"I just wanted you out here, before the branding begins," explained Bayless, passing over a cigar. "And I'm going to ask you, in particular, to watch Bill Longyear. He's here to make trouble, and I know it."

"Oh, Bill's all right," boomed the sheriff jovially as he waved his hand at the crowd. "No harm in Bill— none at all. And if he did happen to start something I could stop him with a word. I'll just go down and get something to eat."

He spurred his horse down the slope and shook

171

hands all around before he stepped down and filled up his plate, and Captain Bayless grunted scornfully. Of course the rustlers had votes, and they had helped elect him sheriff; but Smith Crowder was too friendly, by far. The gang of rustlers was increasing now, their pistols slung with butts straight out to indicate they were prepared for war; and yet the sheriff of the county sat down in the midst of them and filled up his plate with the rest.

"I tell you, Jeff," warned the Captain, "those men are up to mischief. They're organized—better organized than my cowboys—and they're wearing their guns rustler style."

"Wait till you see those brands," laughed Standifer, "and you'll know what's on their minds. I'm sure glad you took that job off my hands."

"Oh, I'm not afraid of them," protested Bayless, "not the least in the world, because I've got my own cowboys behind me. And if I find a mavericked calf sucking a Mill Iron cow I'm going to claim it—and *brand* it."

"That's more like it!" responded Jeff. "Now you're talking my language. And if you get into any trouble, just hold up your hand and I'll come."

"No, no!" protested the boss, "you stay out of this, Jeff. I don't want to have any bloodshed. I'm going to call on Jack to carry out my orders and, my boy, you're going to be surprised."

"Think so?" grinned Standifer. "Well, *you're* liable to be surprised, so you'd better go borrow a gun. I may be wrong, but the first time you claim a calf I look for all hell to break loose."

"For me to carry a gun would just invite a killing," returned the Captain, tugging at his moustache. "Here comes Jack—I'll give him his orders."

He swung up on his horse and trotted off across the cutting ground to where Flagg was holding up the herd, and Standifer remained behind to watch. From the summit of the butte he could see the road from town and also all that happened below him. It was a fine day, clear and bright, and in the crystalline air every face and brand stood out. But if there were any friendly faces in the crowd below they were certainly not turned towards him. They glanced up at him furtively, rustler and cowboy alike, but no one ventured a remark. The story of Shorty Updegraf had got around.

A pandemonium of lowing and bawling broke loose as the huge herd came to a stand. Mothers sought for their lost calves, smelling briefly of each back as blatting orphans came running up to them, then horning them disdainfully away. Angry bulls, pawing and rumbling, plowed their way through the throng, bellowing a challenge as they met one of their kind; and the dust rose up in a cloud. With tossing heads and gleaming eyes the living mass milled and circled, their polished horns catching the sun, and the earth seemed to tremble beneath their feet.

Leaving a few to hold the herd, Jack Flagg and the top hands whom he had selected to do the cutting rode over in a body to the chuck-wagon. They were Texans to a man, long and lanky with double-rigged saddles and a short grass-rope tied to the horn; and as they stepped down they glanced up at Standifer. Then they turned with friendlier mien to Bill Longyear and his rustlers, who sat waiting for the cutting to begin. Perhaps Jeff was mistaken, but it seemed to him that there was some understanding between them.

Gibes and sarcastic yells were bandied to and fro above the organ-like lowing of the herd; and then, bitten by hunger and shaken by their potations, the cowboys poured out coffee and sat down. They ate hugely, drinking cup after cup of coffee to steady their frazzled nerves; and when they rose up and went to change horses the cattle had quieted down. Mothers suckled their calves, the leg-weary ones laid down, the bulls only grumbled their resentment; and off at one side a branding-fire was lit while the cowboys got the irons from the bed-wagon. It was time for the branding to begin.

Mounted on quick, active cutting-horses the range boss and his two helpers rode slowly through the standing herd, marking down the cows with calves. Then, shaking out their ropes, they whipped them down over some calf and dragged him up to the fire. The mother followed frantically and, calling her brand, the roper turned him over to the flankers. Almost like clock-rope they rode in and out, seldom if ever missing a throw; and, master of them all, Jack Flagg was in his glory, the best roper and cowman in the outfit. From the top of the butte, where he had retired to watch the work, Captain Bayless was loud in his praise. But Standifer was reading the brands.

With eyes trained for years to note every iron and ear-mark he scrutinized each cow and calf, and the brands that were burned on with the stamp-irons. All was regular and proper—too regular and too proper, for the herd was full of hair-brands. They were dragging out the good ones first. Beyond the fire in a solid phalanx the jealous-eyed rustlers looked on, ready to protest if a brand was called wrong. They were noisy and turbulent, circulating bottles of whisky to keep up their fighting spirit, but for an hour nothing went wrong.

Standifer leaned against the tree-trunk, checking the branding with side glances while he watched the road from town. Belated cowboys were riding out to join the outfit at the wagons, and among them he rather looked for Shorty. There was something in the wind, some blow-off for which they waited, and he watched every man as he arrived. Some were drunk, but the drunkest of all was a red-headed cowboy whom Jeff had never seen. Standifer thought he was not quite as drunk as he acted.

Whooping and reeling and brandishing a bottle he charged straight into the rustler ranks, insisting upon a drink all around; and then, as if at a signal, Jack Flagg rode out of the herd. On his rope, bucking and bawling, was a big bull calf which had recently been branded Hog Eye. But the cow which followed after it had the Mill Iron on her hip—and Jack Flagg did not hesitate.

"Mill Iron!" he called, passing his slack to a calf-rastler; and the brander picked up his stamp-iron. But

175

Bill Longyear had not been caught napping.

"Hold on, thar!" he shouted, jumping his horse into the midst of them. "That's my calf—cain't you see the brand?"

He pointed at the newly-made Hog Eye but the range boss confronted him angrily.

"There's his mammy," he said. "She's a Mill Iron!"

"I don't give a damn!" retorted Longyear vindictively. "You cain't bar no brand of mine!"

"Oh, I can't, hey?" sneered Flagg, stepping down from his horse; and with a hot iron he crossed out the brand. But before he could clap on a Mill Iron the rustlers spurred to the rescue.

"Come on, Crowder!" called Bayless, swinging up on his horse, "this is nothing but a plain case of stealing. But Jeff, you stay here. Understand?"

"Yes, sir!" responded Standifer, though he had not offered to start; and sheriff and General Manager rode down together, just as Flagg branded the calf and turned it loose.

"There's your calf!" he said to Longyear. "And that's what going to happen to every one that claims a Company cow for its mammy. I've got my orders from the boss!"

"To hell with him!" railed Longyear, shaking out a loop and roping the calf as it fled. "I branded this calf first, on the open range, and no man nor Company can steal him."

He jumped down into the flying dust and hog-tied the calf, keeping up a running fire of abuse. Then as a hot iron was passed to him and the rustlers gathered around he stood astride his prize.

"Don't you dare to burn my brand!" warned Bay-less, rushing in on him, "or I'll have you arrested for grand larceny. This calf was with my cow—"

"He was not—when I branded him!" yapped back Longyear. "He was a maverick, and I found him first. That's the law of the range—the first man that sees him! Bring me a hot iron, boys! He's my calf!"

Men ran to and fro, scuffling and fighting over branding-irons, all shouting and gesticulating at once; but up on the butte the lone Ranger sat unmoved—the battle did not seem quite real. Why should Flagg and Bill Longyear, after drinking together the night before, suddenly fly at each other's throats like angry dogs? And why should rustlers and Company men, as if at a signal, suddenly indulge in all this commotion? That was not the way in which range wars were set-tled—the ultimate appeal was the gun.

He glanced back towards town, still suspicious of some treachery, still watching for Shorty Updegraf to come; when, up from the ford and out across the flats, he saw Annabelle's bay racer, coming fast. Perhaps she had heard of the conflict, or perhaps she was bringing him warning.

A sudden silence smote his ear, after all the noise and shouting, and he looked down to see Bill Longyear beckoning to him.

"Come down hyar, Mr. Ranger," he challenged, waving a smoking iron in the air. "Come down hyar and try to stop me if you think fer a minute I won't put my iron on this calf!"

He paused as cowboy and rustler alike awaited the expected reply, but Standifer only laughed.

"Don't wait on me," he said, "or your iron will get cold. There's the sheriff—talk to him!"

"You're scairt!" scoffed the rustler, still brandishing his iron. "Come down and fight it out, like a man!"

"No, you stay where you are, Jeff!" ordered the Captain from the crowd. "I can attend to this matter myself. And Mistuh Sheriff, I order you, the minute he brands my calf, to place Bill Longyear under arrest."

"All right," jeered Longyear, with another look at Standifer. "I'll jest brand him, then—and dare you to arrest me!"

He reached out for a hot running-iron and, big across the ribs, he ran his rustler brand, the Hog Eye. Jeff started to his feet and hooked his toe into the stirrup. He had not looked for him to go so far. But, instead of arresting him, Smith Crowder held up his hand and tried to make a speech.

"Now here, boys," he began; but the rustlers cut him short with a chorus of scornful blats.

"Go hire a hall!" they shouted, "you can't arrest nobody!" And suddenly the sheriff fell back.

"Arrest that man!" ordered Bayless again; and then he waved his hand for Jeff. His house of cards had fallen, for not a cowboy had offered to help; and rather than accept defeat he appealed to the one man who would fight. The Ranger mounted and rode down slowly.

"Mistuh Standifer," spoke up the Captain, "as a deputy sheriff, I order you to arrest that man." He pointed an accusing finger at the arrogant Rustler King, but Jeff only shrugged his shoulders. This was not his way of doing, at all. With the rustlers drawn up in front and Jack Flagg and his men behind he was penned in and wide open to treachery. And now the rustlers were spoiled.

"Here's the sheriff," he answered shortly. "Give your orders to him. What do you want to do—start a killing!"

He reined his horse away from the crowd and turned back to face them, his eyes on Bill Longyear—and Jack Flagg. The range boss was watching him, sneeringly.

"You're a hell of a detective," he mocked. "I thought a Ranger never turned back!"

"Well, they don't," retorted Jeff, trying to draw him into a fight. "Not from a thieving whelp like you! Pull your gun, and we'll shoot it out!"

"Who—me?" laughed Flagg. "What the hell would I do that for! Why don't you go in and arrest Bill Longyear!"

He was trying to egg him on, to crowd him into a framed-up conflict, and Standifer fought as desperately to avoid it.

"Because," he answered, "you're a worse thief than they are. They work on their own time and go about it openly. But you, you big stiff, draw your pay from the Company and then turn around and rob it. You're a dodrammed thief, and I know it!"

He paused, his eyes flashing dangerously as he faced the grinning range boss; but just as Captain Bayless hurried over between them there was a clatter of hoofs behind. Jeff turned with lightning quickness, his hand on his gun, every nerve set to draw and shoot. But it was Annabelle, riding in at a gallop.

"Jeff!" she called, waving her hand imploringly as she came over the brow of the hill, "come up here, quick! I want to see you."

Standifer turned to Jack Flagg, who was cursing as he watched her, and ran his eye over the crowd. The presence of a woman had broken the fighting tension which was urging them on towards a killing and they stood almost abashed in her presence.

"All right!" he responded genially. "Anything to please a lady." And turning his back on his enemies he rode up to meet her, smiling.

"Come further!" she entreated as she reined in beside him and stared back at the sullen crowd. "*Please,* Jeff!" And she leaned over closer. "They're planning to kill you—I know it!" she whispered. But Standifer only laughed.

"I know that," he said, riding off with her the while. "Just waiting for the break, when you came."

"But listen, Jeff!" she insisted. "Did you notice that red-headed cowboy? No, don't look—he was sent out to kill you!"

Standifer glanced back involuntarily, but she whipped in between them and the look in her eyes made him grave.

"I saw him," she panted, "practicing the draw, back in that alley. He's going to shoot you, right now!"

"Oh, I guess not," responded Jeff, "now that I know

180

who it is." And he whipped his rifle up out of its scabbard.

"No!" she said. "Don't stop here—they'll kill you. Oh, Jeff, haven't I earned something, by this? Then ride over the hill with me as if we were just talking, and get away, while there's time!"

Standifer glanced back over his shoulder, seeking a red head in the seething crowd, then thrust the gun back into its scabbard.

"It's a nice day for a ride, Annabelle," he suggested. And with a touch of the spurs they were gone.

CHAPTER XXII
Rustlers' Roost

THEY WENT OVER the top of the butte and down the other side in a wild and breath-taking gallop; but Annabelle sat her horse with the ease of an Arab, looking back and laughing as they raced. Her blooded bay had taken the lead, and Standifer let her keep it while he watched the hills behind. But no one came riding after them, not even the red-headed cowboy.

In the furor and excitement Jeff had completely forgotten him, and his pretense of being too drunk; but now he saw plainly that the cowboy's arrival had been the signal for dragging out the calf. Jack Flagg and Bill Longyear had been working together to lure him into a fight. They had staged the whole quarrel to cap Standifer into it and give their killer a chance to shoot. How easy it would have been, at the first crack of a gun, for Red to have shot him from behind! And who could prove, if any tried, which shot in a hundred had sent the lone Ranger to his death?

A cold sweat beaded Jeff's brow as he realized how close it had been, and there flashed up before his eyes the twisted lips of Jack Flagg, cursing his luck that Annabelle had come. But for her interference and the high-handed way in which she had snatched him away, the conspirators would have wiped him out. He would have been shot down, mysteriously, and the bold plot of the rustlers would have been carried out, undisturbed. But what a fool he had been to let the Captain and Smith Crowder draw him down into that crowd of killers! They were fools to have tried it, and he was a greater one to have yielded, but now he had learned his lesson.

"Come on!" coaxed Annabelle as Jeff lagged and looked back, uneasy over the plight of Bayless; and her smile was so wistful that he followed without a word until they came to an isolated butte. "Now up to the top!" she cried, "where nobody can get near us. I want to tell you something important!"

On its smooth, flat summit she dropped down, panting, her eyes big with suppressed excitement.

"Who do you think I saw with him?" she demanded. "A man you'd never guess! But first you've got to make me a promise!"

"Sure! Sure!" agreed Standifer. "Anything you say, Annabelle! Who was the doggoned scoundrel?"

"Now don't forget!" she charged. "You've made me a promise! Anything that I say—you've got to do it!

Sit down, and I'll begin at the beginning."

She led the way to the natural seat on the edge of the rim, where they could look out the country below, and Standifer followed, impatiently.

"I was so scared!" she sighed. "When I woke up this morning I knew something terrible would happen. And when you rode by without even looking up at me I was so nervous I just had to do something. So I watched the street, and that alley behind, until I saw Red, under a shed. He was standing with his pistol out sideways, on his hip—and Jeff, he was practicing the draw!"

"Getting his hand in," nodded Standifer. "But how'd you know he was laying for me?"

"He was drunk," shuddered Annabelle, "and every time he drew he said 'I'm going to kill the'—and he called you a bad name."

"I bet you!" grinned Jeff. "They all call me bad names. But there are other blankety-blanks in the world."

"But this other man came out and spoke to Red 'Shut up!' he said, 'you'll give the whole snap away.' And Red answered back, real loud. 'Well, if that detective is as fast as they say he is, I need a little practice, first.' "

"That settles it," admitted Standifer. "And it's a lucky thing for me you overheard him. Now who was this man that called him?"

"It was Judge Schmaltz," stated Annabelle. "The Justice of the Peace. I could hardly believe my ears!"

"Holy smoke!" exclaimed Jeff, "that explains a

whole lot of things. I'll bet you every officer in this county has been bought up, while they pull off this mammoth steal!"

"Very likely," smiled Annabelle. "But now you'll have to pay me for being such a good detective. Haven't I lived up to my position as a Texas Ranger's wife! Well, I've always wanted the pleasure of a gallop across the prairie with you. Come on, Jeff—let's ride and ride!"

"I'll go you!" agreed Standifer, with a glance towards the cutting-ground. "And in this case the pleasure is mine. I believe a nice long ride would be good for my health, the way things are breaking, over east."

He nodded towards the butte, where a company of horsemen had come in sight, headed for town. In the lead rode Smith Crowder, huge and mountainous on his horse, with Bill Longyear, apparently a prisoner. And in the rear of the party of rustlers which followed them up rode Red, the cowboy killer.

"The treacherous whelp!" muttered Jeff, "I'll put a torch under him that will run him clear, out of the country."

"No you won't," said Annabelle. "You made me a promise, and here's what you've got to do. You must keep out of town until all these men have left. Now come on for a long, long ride!"

She mounted, unaided, and as they sat their horses they saw Red rein in and look. He started towards them, slowly, then changed his mind and galloped off after the rest.

"He's wise," observed Standifer. "He knows that we've twigged him and he'd only run into a bullet. But I'm going to keep that promise and stay out of his way. And now, Mrs. Standifer, we'll ride!"

He jumped his horse down off the cap-rock and they rode towards the river, smiling happily, never looking back. It was the first time in their lives that they had ever been together, free from prying, watchful eyes. What they said and did would never be noted and passed on from gossip to gossip. They were themselves, at last, and Annabelle rode close beside him, for had he not called her Mrs. Standifer? But the sun sank low at last and they turned back, reluctantly, until at dusk they rode down to the crossing.

"Good-bye, Jeff," she said, as they halted by the ford. "And stay away from Jack—will you promise!"

"Promise anything!" he answered lightly, "to keep peace in the family. Better tell 'em I've skipped the country, Annabelle."

"Oh, can I?" she cried. "They'll all think so, anyhow. But you'll come back—won't you, Jeff?"

"Yes—and that's a promise, too," he answered huskily. "I think a lot of you, Annabelle."

"Well, I just love you!" exclaimed Annabelle impulsively. And she took his hand, gazing up at him wistfully. He watched from the shore as she forded the muddy river and waved a glove at him gaily. Then he reined back into the darkness that was settling on the plain, riding slowly, his head bowed in thought. All their anger had left them, and the eternal quarrels about posing as husband and wife. They had found peace at last, where there was no peace—peace and friendship in the midst of war. But he had not asked for a kiss.

He had a mission to fulfill and a debt to pay, for the last of his doubts was dispelled. Jack Flagg and his men, Bill Longyear and his rustlers, were in conspiracy to take his life. They had hired a second killer when Shorty Updegraf had weakened, and only a miracle had saved him. But for the intervention of Annabelle he would have been drawn into a shooting and Red would have earned his money. But now they had failed, and like the rolling back of a scroll their sordid scheme had been revealed.

It was revenge that called him now, a stern anger against the enemies who valued their stealings above a man's life: Such creatures were dangerous, a menace to society, the kind of scum that the Rangers had always battled with; and, hunted and alone, he took a vow never to stop till he landed the last man in jail. And if the jail would not hold them, if the sheriff had gone over to them, he would shoot it out, man to man.

A wolfish cunning came over him as he rode out into the night, and for four days he hid like a criminal, living meagerly on company beef. Others were killing cattle, too, the very men that he hunted; and as he lurked in the cedar-brakes he saw the rustlers on the plains, driving their stolen calves up into the hills. Every canyon was Rustlers' Roost.

Hiding by day and prowling by night he beheld at first hand the saturnalia of wholesale theft—cowboys out on the circle throwing back unbranded calves, or those that were sleepered and hair-branded. And at night, like prowling coyotes, their allies the rustlers, gathering the calves and driving them off. In all that wide country there seemed no man to restrain them—not one honest man to say them nay.

Worn out and disgusted, starved down on his diet of straight beef, Standifer turned back at last under cover of the dark, and slipped into town from the north. All was quiet now, for rustlers and cowboys were working day and night on the range. Only a few drunken roisterers raised their voices from the saloons, and the jail was as dead as a tomb. Jeff scouted round and round, peering in through doors and windows, until at last by the one dim light he discovered the sheriff in his office, sleeping peacefully in his big, stuffed chair.

What a sheriff he was, never leaving the town except to round up more votes! And when he did go out and become a witness to their stealing, turning back at the first rustler snarl. They would rend him like wolves if he broke in on their business or sought to prevent them from pulling down their prey, and Standifer shared their contempt. He strode in noisily, rousing him up from his slumbers, and Crowder stared back at him, blinking.

"Well, what are *you* doing here?" he demanded. "I thought you'd left the country!"

"Nope—sorry to disappoint you," answered Jeff. "What's doing? How did you come out with Longyear?"

"W'y, that dodrammed, drunken justice of the peace turned him loose!" raged Crowder, rearing up from his

187

chair. "He claimed, by grab, that Bill had seen the maverick first. Claimed his brand was what counted, no matter what his mammy's was! What chance has a sheriff got of enforcing the law if this JP is going to turn 'em all loose? I done quit—no use wasting your time!"

"Well, he's not the only JP in the county," returned Jeff. "What's the matter with that Mormon, up at Moab? He'd hold 'em for the Grand Jury, and I know it."

"No use stirring up trouble," grumbled the sheriff morosely. "Although them Mormons are good and sore. And by the way, while I think about it, there's a telegram here for you. Came down over the military line. But we thought you'd left—your wife practically admitted it—so I opened it up, myself."

He pawed about his desk until, under some old papers, he unearthed the three-days-old message.

"It ain't signed," he complained, "and I couldn't make no sense out of it. The boys all thought you'd quit."

He handed over the yellow paper and Jeff scanned it briefly while the sheriff waited, expectantly.

"Come to Moab. Remember your promise," it read; and Standifer folded it grimly.

"Don't you think it," he said. "I haven't quit—I've just begun." And he rushed out to hunt up Rover.

CHAPTER XXIII
A Cold Trail

THE UNSIGNED TELEGRAM was a message from Bishop Lillywhite, and the promise which Jeff had given him was to arrest the first Gentile that the Mormons caught stealing their cows. It was a promise which, in his present mood, he was more than glad to live up to, no matter who the rustlers were. But first he must find Rover and get him out of town, without revealing his own presence to his enemies. Now that the rustlers counted him gone they would throw caution to the winds and indulge in an orgy of stealing. He ducked down the alley after Rover.

Every crate and tin can in that ungraceful passageway was stamped on his mind with all the detail of a photographic plate. Here was the barrel, overflowing with bottles, behind which Shorty had crouched, ready to shoot him while he bandied words with Flagg. And there was the darkened shed where Red had practiced the draw, when Annabelle had looked down and seen him. It was a place with a gruesome history of murder and savage brawls and Jeff kept in the deepest shadows while he listened behind the Bucket of Blood.

Here, if anywhere, Ralph the Rover would be holding forth in that big voice which carried so far. Drunk or sober, flush or broke, he made it his headquarters; and presently Jeff heard him speak.

189

"Shut up!" he barked, "or I'll shut you up! Go on, now, and leave me alone!"

There was a murmur of apology, a scornful grunt from Ralph the Rover, and then he was heard no more. Standifer knew his mood well—he was sobering up from a big drunk—but he could not ride south without him. For lack of a side-partner he had all but met his death in the battle at the cutting-grounds, and if the Mormon Bishop put them on the trail of the rustlers he would need the stalwart Rover and his gun. Never in all his life had he found a man more valiant, or more faithful in the hour of need. He crouched down behind the barrel which had sheltered Shorty Updegraf and waited for Rover to come out.

Men stalked to and fro, slamming the back door as they passed, honest drinkers who feared no treachery; and then, down the alley, there came another man who kept in the shadows like a cat. At the door of the Bucket of Blood he paused to listen intently, and when Rover spoke up again he crouched. It was Red, the hired killer of the rustlers. Jeff drew his gun and stepped forth.

"Are you looking for someone?" he challenged; and the startled cowboy whirled and faced him.

"No!" he mumbled, turning swiftly away; and Jeff whipped out his second gun.

"Well, I'm looking for you—you murdering whelp!" he cursed. "Now git!" And he shot up the ground beneath his feet.

Red yelled and struck out running with Standifer close behind him, emptying his pistols in a rattling fusillade. Then Jeff ducked into a doorway, loading his guns with lightning speed, and the crowd in the saloon poured forth.

"Who's killed? What's going on?" they clamored in a chorus; and at sight of Red, still legging it up the alley, they took after him with a rush. Whether he fled from sudden death or pursued some hidden enemy was more than the loungers knew, but they took up the hue-and-cry; and, last of all but running strong, came Ralph the Rover himself.

"Here!" exclaimed Standifer, stepping out from behind a shed and laying a rough hand on his shoulder, "where the hell are you going, Rover?"

"What's the matter? Who's shooting?" demanded Rover, stopping short. "Well, by grab, if it ain't you, Jeff!"

"Sure is," responded Standifer, "and I need you, right now. Come over here, where the gang won't see me."

"I thought you'd gone!" protested Rover, as they took shelter across the street. "Well, you've certainly raised merry hell."

"I was smoking up that cowboy the rustlers hired to kill me. Listen there—he's running yet!"

"Did you wing him?" demanded Rover eagerly. "By Gad, Jeff, I'm shore glad to see you!"

"Nope—might've shot a heel off. And I'm glad to see you, Rover. The Bishop wired he'd located some rustlers."

"W'y, the old skeezicks!" shrilled Rover. "Are you going out after them? Just wait till I get my horse."

He led the way between buildings to the high fence of the O.K. Corral and leapt over it with a joyous yip.

"Hell's bells!" he chuckled. "They've been riding me for a week—them fool rustlers think you've skipped the country!"

"They're going to be surprised, when we ride up on 'em," predicted Standifer. "And the first man that draws a gun is due to stop a bullet. They ganged me, out at the cutting-grounds!"

"The murdering whelps—I wish I'd been there!" complained Rover. "But they slipped some knock-out drops into my liquor."

"That's all right," consoled Jeff. "It's a good thing you wasn't or we'd've had a regular killing. But I've got through monkeying with the Captain and his pets—after this we work by ourselves."

"Keno!" applauded Rover, leading out his horse; and half an hour later they galloped out of town and splashed across the ford towards Moab. The time for talking had passed and they rode on in silence, watching the stars as they swung towards the west; until, just at daylight, they rode up to the Bishop's house and summoned him to the door.

"What? You here?" he challenged as he looked them over, blinking. "I'd given you up, long ago. But ride out behind the barn, boys, before somebody sees you." And he went back to stamp on his boots.

"Now!" he began as he hurried out after them. "Do you know that the Mill Iron cowboys are stealing our calves again?"

"They're stealing everybody's," responded Standifer, "the Company's worst of all."

"I doubt that," returned the Bishop cynically. "But I'm glad you kept your word, and here's what I'm going to do. I'm going to put you on the trail where over a hundred calves were driven by here at night. It's old now, of course; but you follow it up and I'll venture you'll cut a fresh one. And then, if you don't weaken, you'll come to some weaning-pens. But don't tell them I showed you the way."

"I'll tell 'em nothing," promised Jeff, "except where they head in at. And much obliged, Bishop, for the tip. Now how about a little breakfast?"

Lillywhite hesitated and scratched his head, for hospitality is the cardinal virtue of the Mormons.

"I'll bring it out to you," he decided. "Because every man has his enemies, you know. Now ride down this lane and I'll meet you across the ditch." And he hustled them out of town.

"The old boy is shore skeered," observed Rover, smiling wickedly. "Reckon the rustlers would make it hot for him, if they knew. But at the same time I can see he's got blood in his eye. All I hope is he don't forget that grub."

They took shelter in the willows that grew along the wide ditch and presently, on his old farm-horse, the Bishop came riding, a flour-sack of food under his arm.

"Here's your breakfast, boys," he said, "and some bread and jerked beef, to last you till you come to their camp. And now ride up this canyon as fast as you can—because I don't want to appear in this at all."

He led the way up a narrow trail that took them over the ridge and down into a deeper canyon beyond; and among the wash boulders they saw the tracks of driven cattle, with shod horse-tracks following behind.

"There it is, boys," said the Bishop; and he reined his old horse around to go.

"Here, hold on!" spoke up Standifer. "I want to ask you a question. What about the JP in this town—can I depend on him to hold my prisoners?"

"If they're Gentiles—you can!" responded the Bishop; and rode away, muttering in his beard.

CHAPTER XXIV
The Maverick Makers

THE COLD TRAIL of the rustlers led up a rocky canyon and on into a rough, volcanic country. Great overflows of lava had formed mesas covered with pines whose roots sucked up water from deep fissures, but the canyon-bed itself was dry as a bone and the Rangers had no canteen. They spurred on doggedly until, at the base of a high mountain, the canyon opened up into a valley; and where a new trail came in they found a crippled cow, limping painfully over the rocks.

"Toes are clipped," observed Rover as the cow faced them resentfully; and Standifer looked up and down the trail.

"Must have a calf, up ahead," he nodded. "These

rustlers are sure picking 'em green."

"Yes, and that's a Mormon brand," added Rover. "Remember what he said about a weaning-pen? These rascals have been driving off the Bishop's calves and filing down their mammies' feet. We're up against a hard outfit, Jeff."

"I believe you're right," agreed Standifer as he rode over to the new trail and scanned the fresh tracks in the dust. "And what's more, they're not far away. We'd better take to the brush."

He led the way up a rocky point and along the rim of a broad mesa that ran parallel to the mountain for miles. The valley lay between them and far ahead, against the sky, they could make out a film of dust. The vagrant wind brought down snatches of a distant turmoil—calves bawling, the high mooing of cows—and as they worked forward from point to point they came in sight of a round valley, with a pole corral in the middle. It was the rendezvous of the maverick makers, most despicable of all cow-thieves, and Rover spat out an oath as he watched.

"The dirty whelps!" he complained. "What the hell are they working here for, when the plains are lousy with mavericks? But no, they've got to file them cows' hoofs down to the quick and run off their sucking calves!"

"They're out to get 'em all," returned Standifer. "Their side-kickers are branding the mavericks. But if our luck holds good we'll round up this prize outfit and slam 'em behind the bars."

"Bore 'em and plant 'em, is more like it," grumbled

Rover. "What's the use of taking chances? Didn't they cap you into a fight and hire a killer to down you? Well, git onto yourself, you poor yap!"

"I know it!" acknowledged Jeff. "But I just want to show 'em I can ketch 'em, like we did those Mexicans. I want to show 'em, by grab, that they ain't worth the powder it would take to blow 'em to hell. And when we get 'em in jail I'll bring down those Moab Mormons and they'll swear the whole outfit into the Pen. That'll break 'em of robbing widows."

"Yes, but how are you going to do it?" objected Rover. "I'm perishing, Jeff, for a drink."

"You'll live," predicted Standifer. "And they must have some water. So we'll watch 'em, and go down at night."

They rode forward through the cedars that crowned the flat-topped mesa until the noise of the round-up was close. Then, tying their fagged horses, they crept up to the rim and looked down into the valley below. It was a sandy patch of grass-land, surrounded by heavy pines; and almost beneath them they could see the top of a tent where the rustlers had made their camp. A boggy place on the edge of the flat marked the presence of a spring and Ralph the Rover sighed and spit dry.

"Let's kill the ornery hounds, and get a drink," he said. "Look at that, now!" And he thrust out his gun.

A burly rustler had left the dust of the chowdered-up corral and ridden over to the hidden spring. They gazed down at him enviously as he knelt to drink, but when he threw off his hat Standifer saw that his hair was red. It was Bill Longyear, the Rustler King.

"Lemme bore him!" pleaded Rover as Jeff pushed his gun aside. "Don't you believe in Divine Providence, or nothing? Ain't the good Lord fetched him up to me, jest on purpose to be kilt? Be reasonable, Jeff—he's going!"

"Let him go!" ordered Standifer. "He's the very man I'm looking for. Wouldn't shoot him for a thousand dollars. Now you stop spitting cotton and let me watch this outfit a while and I'll show you how the Texan Rangers work."

"You'll play hell," retorted Rover scornfully. "Don't the Rangers ever eat or drink? And what's the use of ketching him—won't the jury turn him loose? Dang it, Jeff, your brains have baked."

Standifer stretched out in the shade of a scanty cedar and watched the unconscious rustlers below him. He was not three hundred yards from where they roped and branded—but to shoot would be to start a war. If they killed Bill Longyear, the chief of the rustlers, and scattered the rest of his band, the news would spread like wildfire until every canyon and cabin gave up its fighting men. They were organized and ready for just such a call, and Jeff and Rover would never escape alive. They were two men against hundreds and the only strength that upheld them was the hidden arm of the law. They were officers, and the government stood behind them.

By the fire in a smother of dust and heat four men, besides Longyear, were toiling. They rode out by turns among the bawling cows and calves that circled the makeshift pen, and after making their throw they dragged their catch to the fire and worked over the ears and brand. Unconscious that they were watched they did not even look up at the frowning rim of lava above them. This valley had been their hold-out, perhaps for many years, never entered by officers of the law; and now, in the heyday of their harvest, they worked until the sun sunk low. Then one man came out and rode off up a canyon returning just at dusk.

"There's the weaning-pen, I'll bet ye," suggested Rover. "The old Bishop said they had one. Let's go up there, when it gets good and dark!"

"Nope, we'll hide here a while," decided Standifer. "I don't want them to find our tracks." And not until midnight would he submit to Rover's pleadings and venture up to the spring. They rode in bareback, hanging low, Comanche fashion, and dropped down to get a drink. Then, dragging out their tracks, they returned to the barren mesa and another long, thirsty day. Ralph the Rover had been raised an Indian, learning their stoical endurance; but as the heat beat down on them and Jeff waited on stubbornly he broke out into new complaints.

"Look at that rustler king!" he railed as Bill Longyear rode by below them. "By grab, I could shoot all his buttons off. I'm going crazy with the heat, and I'm shore liable to do it, too. What the devil are you waiting for, anyway?"

"Never mind," answered Standifer. "They're three to one, ain't they? Play Injun, and see what happens."

But nothing happened, except that one man rode up the canyon and came back, as before, just at dusk.

"You're right, Rover," said Jeff. "Up there is their weaning-pen. And tomorrow, if that jasper goes out again—"

"We'll ketch him!" nodded Rover. And so they waited.

At night, riding in like horses coming to water, they drank deep and returned to their hiding-place. But though they still had food from the Bishop's supply, to eat was to add to their thirst. So they starved and in the morning the party of rustlers broke up, leaving three to guard the camp. All their calves had been marked and branded and Bill Longyear with two hands rode back down the trail towards the plains. Rover followed him with his rifle, holding a bead as he passed, begging brokenly for permission to shoot, but Standifer shook his head.

Here was the outlet for cattle stolen or thrown back by the cowboys as they made their great circles on the plain; and it was reasonable to suppose that Bill Longyear would come back, since he was the chief of the gang. And, with him out of the valley, their vigilance would relax—at last they could strike a blow. Shortly after noon the lone cowboy mounted his horse and rode away up the mountain canyon, and as the valley became still Jeff and Rover picked up their rifles and went back down the trail on foot.

An hour afterwards, scouting along beneath the trees, they passed the sleeping camp and turned off up the canyon, walking noiselessly, pausing to look at each turn. A low blatting of calves came down the wind and they quit the dusty trail. Then, creeping in like Indians, they topped the ridge above and saw the calves, peacefully cropping the young grass. They were small and rough-haired, gaunted down by the long drive and starving for their mothers' milk; but in the short time that was allowed them outside the pen they were filling their stomachs full.

Long and patiently, from the heights, the two Rangers reconnoitered the canyon until at last, by the shaded spring, they discovered the lone rustler, lying flat on his back, asleep. As silent as shadows they glided from tree to tree, but as they crept in upon him the cowboy roused up and glanced about at the calves.

Then, idly, he picked up stones and chucked them into the water, while Rover whispered a curse, with dry lips. Still patiently, still silently, they moved up from tree to tree; and then, at his elbow, Standifer spoke.

"Hello!" he said, rising up; and the rustler almost fell into the spring.

"W'y, w'y—who are you?" he stammered, gazing from one to the other, never thinking of the pistol at his hip; and Standifer began trying him out.

"We're out hunting," he said, "and we got lost. Have you got any grub around here?"

"Not a bean!" lied the rustler, still watching them. And suddenly his expression changed. He knew who they were, these gaunt rough-bearded men who stood watching him with still, mirthless eyes, and he blinked and glanced down the trail.

"Got a camp down below?" inquired Jeff. And once more the rustler lied, desperately.

"Well, gimme a drink of water!" broke in Rover. "What the hell are you living on—air?"

He dented his hat-rim and scooped water into it, never taking his eyes from the cowboy; and when he had finished he straightened up with a sigh.

"Try some," he said to Jeff; and while Standifer drank he took charge of the uneasy prisoner.

"Ain't I seen you before, somewhere?" he asked, cocking his head with a knowing grin. "Seems like your face is familiar."

"Oh, he knows you," jested Standifer. "Only he won't admit it. I've seen him—down in Bitterwater."

"No, suh, I never been thar," protested the rustler. "I jest came out from Texas."

"You hear that?" laughed Jeff, turning to Rover. "Here's one of your old side-kicks, I'll bet!"

"Ump-umm!" denied Rover. "Never seen him before. I have to be careful of my reputation."

"Yes, you're a damned good brand-burner," admitted Standifer. "And this gentleman here, as near as I can make out, is only a common calf-weaner. Some nester's kid I reckon, but he looks too fat and sassy for a man that's plumb out of grub."

"Oh, he's got some," spoke up Rover, "and a good camp, to boot. Only he's too danged mean and ornery to feed us."

"No, I haven't," insisted the rustler. And Jeff drew his pistol, while Rover stepped suddenly aside.

"Now, here," began Standifer, "there's no use lying

201

to us, because we know all about you, Tuffy. You've got a camp right down below here and you'd better take us to it, before—"

"We fill you full of holes!" ended Rover.

For a moment the rustler hesitated, his face a ghastly white, and then he hung his head.

"Unbuckle that gun-belt," ordered Jeff. "And lead us into camp," he added.

"All right," faltered the cowboy, "you've got me. Only don't let that man thar kill me."

He glanced fearfully at Rover, who snatched away his pistol and gave him a start down the trail.

"You lousy whelp!" he cursed. "Don't look sad-eyed at me or I'll boot you clean into town. Now you take us into camp and tell those jaspers there that we're your particular friends. Understand? And another thing, Willie. At the first crooked move—"

"Down comes your meat-house," ended Jeff.

They glanced at each other knowingly and followed along behind the rustler's horse, until they came in sight of camp. Dusk had fallen in the deep valley and the two men by the camp-fire could not see the wary Rangers as they approached. All they noticed was their partner, returning from the weaning-pen, and they did not give him a second glance. Yet they were men that Rover knew for desperate characters, these hard-faced, saturnine rustlers; and Standifer took no chances. He carried his rifle cocked and as they came close to the fire he stepped aside and dropped down on one knee. Even then they only stared, so complete was their surprise, and Ralph the Rover did the honors.

"Good evening, gentlemen," he hailed, letting go of the horse's tail and stepping out jauntily to the front. "Howdy, Tate! Hello, Harry! You've got company."

He cocked his rifle noisily and Tate Bascom turned pale, but the other looked around for his gun.

"Put your hands up!" ordered Standifer, "or I'll kill you like a rattlesnake." And reluctantly they obeyed his command.

"Fine and dandy!" nodded Rover. "You shore showed good judgment. Because that gentleman behind the gun is Cap Bayless' Texas Ranger, and he can hit the thin edge of a dime."

He walked out grinning and unhooked Tate's belt, collecting Harry's weapons as he passed.

"That's all, Jeff," he called, glancing into the tent; and Standifer walked into camp. Without firing a shot they had captured three desperate rustlers, but already Tate had got back his nerve.

"You'll sing a different tune," he said to Rover, "when the boys ketch onto your game. Don't you never think you'll leave here alive. But go ahead— have a good time."

He held out his wrists for the loop that Rover was tying and with practiced hands Rover bound them, one by one, and dragged them over against a log. Then while Jeff searched the tent he tilted the cover of a Dutch-oven and shook their blackened coffeepot.

"W'y, Willie," he said reproachfully, "you lied to me like hell when you said you were out of grub. Here's some nice bread and coffee and a big pot of beans. And gentlemen, I've got room for it all."

He patted his stomach and filled up a plate, while the rustler they called Willie grunted. But he too had his hopes.

"You wait until the boys blow in," he said; and Standifer nodded grimly.

"Expecting Bill?" he asked. "Well, that's good news for us. And don't you ever think that we're afraid of a little shooting. We came out here looking for war."

"Yes, and the first thing I'll do," went on Rover, "when Bill Longyear and the boys open up, will be to hunch down behind that log. Tie you rascals down tight and shoot out between you. We've worked that scheme, before."

"You'll never take us to jail," stated Tate Bascom confidently. "And if you do they'll turn us loose. So go ahead, while you're lucky. Because before you git through you'll find that your name is Mud."

"Yes, and yours will be Beef, if you talk back to me," railed Rover. "Think I'll let you fellows go? Well, I may turn you loose, but before you git away I'll shoot you where your galluses cross."

He made a face and grinned wickedly and as the night came on he bound the prisoners, hand and foot. Their own throwropes, pliant and stretched from jerking down cows, served to bind them fast to the log; and while they waited in sullen silence Rover mounted the rustler's horse and galloped down to bring back their own.

"Heard Bill coming," he announced as he stepped into the firelight. "Bringing in another bunch of calves. He's going to be surprised that you boys don't come and help; but we need you in our business, don't we, Jeff?"

He crouched down behind them and thrust out his gun, and Standifer nodded confidently.

"You stay right there," he said. "And shoot the first man that draws. I'll take care of Mr. Longyear, myself."

He threw some wood on the fire, to make a steady blaze when the rustlers rode into view, and stepped into the shadow of the pines. The others had been easy, but Bill Longyear was redheaded and he had two men at his back. They came in slowly, whooping and slapping their chaps, lashing the drags as the tired calves lagged; but no one rode out to help. Bill Longyear was cursing mad but he could not leave the herd until at last they put up the bars. Then he rode back, muttering, unsuspecting of any danger, until he entered the light of the fire.

Ralph the Rover rose up, a pistol in each hand, his hat pulled down over his eyes, and Longyear jerked back his horse.

"What the hell are you doing?" he yapped.

"Ketching snipes," answered Rover. "Put 'em up!"

Longyear turned to the two cowboys who had ridden up behind him and looked again at the three men against the log.

"By Gad," he exclaimed as he caught sight of the ropes. "It's a hold-up!" And he reached for his gun.

"Be-e careful!" warned Rover, bringing his pistols to a point; and suddenly Longyear knew him.

"You Company spy!" he cursed, swinging down

205

behind his horse. But as he reined him away and sunk the spurs into his flanks another man rose before him. It was Standifer, and the rustler stopped. His rowelled horse was fighting his head and bucking to escape, but Longyear yanked him cruelly back. Not a word was said, but three pairs of hands went up and Standifer took their guns.

"Why didn't you draw?" he taunted. But Longyear only laughed.

"Ump-umm!" he said. "And give you a chance to kill me? That would be playing right into your hand!"

CHAPTER XXV
The "Fight Outfit"

WITH THEIR SIX prisoners in a row, bound fast by their own ropes which had pulled down many a cow, the two Rangers stood guard through the night. But at the first peep of dawn Jeff sent Rover to wrangle the horses and they took the long trail home. Tying their mounts head and tail they drove the rustlers before them until they entered the settlement of Moab; and there, meeting the Bishop, they inquired for the justice of the peace.

"What the hell are you up to?" demanded Longyear, who so far had uttered no complaint. "Thar's a JP right in Bitterwater, and you know it."

"Well, what's the matter with this one?" inquired Standifer. "He might turn the whole bunch of you loose."

"Yes, and then again," said Longyear, "he might not. I don't want to be tried by no Mormon!"

"The law says," went on Jeff, "that men arrested for a felony shall be examined before the nearest justice of the peace. And if not held they shall be released from custody."

"Well, go ahead," grumbled Longyear. "No use looking for justice here. I can see you've got it all framed."

"I've never seen this judge in my life," answered Standifer. And the Bishop regarded him grimly. No sign of recognition had passed between them, but he knew that his secret was safe. So he led the way to the office of the Mormon justice, where after a brief examination they were held for the Grand Jury and their bail fixed at five thousand dollars.

"Five thousand!" yelped Longyear. "I'm a pore man, Judge, and the Grand Jury won't sit for four months!"

"You should have thought of that," said the judge, "before you stole these cattle. Court's adjourned!" And he waved them away.

Spurring doggedly down the trail, on the lookout for pursuit or the least sign of treachery among his prisoners, Standifer hardly drew rein until, late that afternoon, he lodged them in the county jail. A crowd collected instantly, Smith Crowder rushed upon him and assailed him with a hundred excited questions; but, leaving Rover to watch the rustlers, Jeff hurried into the courthouse and sought out the district attorney.

Here was one man he could trust, or thought he

could trust, to aid him in getting a conviction. That was his duty, as representative of The People—but when Standifer mentioned the names of the men he had arrested he noticed a subtle change. When he had prosecuted the Mexicans, and Ike Cutbrush the Mormon butcher, Sutton had gone at it like a fighting cock. Now his hackles were down and he only looked gravely interested, with something else on his mind.

"What evidence have you got?" he asked, and instinctively Jeff began to hedge. It came over him suddenly that not two weeks before Bill Longyear had been arrested—and released. Smith Crowder had brought him in, and Schmaltz had turned him loose. Did the rustlers number Sutton among their friends?

"Well, I'll tell you," he began, "I've got the evidence to convict, and I'm going back to get more. But before I start out I want to be sure that these men won't be released on bail. The JP up at Moab fixed their bail at five thousand and it's your job to fight a motion to reduce."

"Five thousand!" repeated Sutton. "On a grand larceny charge? It seems to me that's excessive!"

"Well, it is," conceded Jeff. "But do you want these men turned loose, to run all my witnesses out of the country? How the devil can we convict them—or do you want to convict? Yes or no—I don't give a damn!"

"Why, certainly!" protested Sutton. "But please remember, Mr. Standifer, you are not the district attorney! And since Longyear, for instance, was arrested only last week it might look like malicious persecution. The Grand Jury, as you know, will not be called for several months—unless we ask for a special session—"

"Well, ask for it, then, unless you want to see this county torn wide open by a rustler war. Because I'll tell you right now I'll protest to the district judge if you try to lower that bail. I've risked my life to bring Bill Longyear to trial, and he's known as the Rustler King. If you turn him loose and let him jump his bail—"

"Mr. Standifer!" barked Sutton, rising up, "you are going entirely too far. Don't you dare even to intimate that I would so far forget my duty as to let a guilty man escape!"

"All right!" flared back Jeff. "I won't intimate anything. But if those men are not in jail when I get back from the mountains I'll hold you responsible, personally!"

He left the office abruptly, without waiting for a reply, and went back to Ralph the Rover.

"Listen, Rover," he said when he had drawn him aside, "we've got the big bear by the ears and we don't dare to let him go. Now you watch him, savvy, while I bring in those calves—and don't let them dope your whisky!"

"Oh, murder!" complained Rover. "And me dying for a drink! But all right—only you hurry right back!"

"I'll do it," promised Jeff. "And before I go I'll bring you a quart of the best. But that district attorney has thrown in with the rest of them, and they're trying to turn Longyear loose."

"Why don't you speak to Cap Bayless?" suggested Rover.

"It's no use," grumbled Standifer. "He said once he'd give me a thousand dollars if I'd hang Bill's hide on the fence. But if I'd go back to him now it would be nothing but Jack Flagg, and what an honest, reliable range boss he was."

"Yes, the dirty whelp," scoffed Rover. "And him out-stealing them all. Only he's too danged slick—we can't ketch him."

"I'll get him!" gritted Jeff. "When I finish up with Longyear. Now, who's a good man to take back with me for a witness—and to help round up those calves? A man that's well known and respected by everybody, and never told a lie in his life?"

"Frank Turnbull!" answered Rover instantly. "The only honest cowman in the country. You tell him what you want and if he undertakes the job at all he'll stay with you till hell's no more. His ranch is over west there, 'bout twenty miles from Rustlers' Canyon. But don't tell him I sent you, Jeff!"

"Yes, I will, Rover," responded Standifer, wringing his hand. "You're the best friend I've got in the country. I'll tell him you sent me and I'll bet that thousand dollars he admits you're a damned good man."

"Well, he might," admitted Rover, as they parted. "Good man at drinking whisky—and don't you forget that bottle! But the old man keeps a black book for every cow-thief in this county, and I reckon my name is thar!"

He grinned, and Jeff was scrupulous to bring back

the bottle before he changed horses and slipped out of town. There was no time now for a visit with Annabelle, no time to eat or drink or change clothes. They had the bear by the ears and they could not let him go—he rode hard, until far into the night.

The round-up cook of the FIT outfit had just beaten on his dishpan for breakfast when a lone rider appeared and, after the custom of the country, filled his plate at the ovens and sat down. Nothing was said by anybody, for old Frank I. Turnbull expected his hands to eat, not talk. From daylight to dark was all too short a time for the riding he had to do, and already it was light enough to rope. But while his men were catching their horses he walked over to the stranger and fixed him with a penetrating eye.

"Were you looking for somebody?" he asked.

"Yes, sir," responded Jeff, rising up. "I'm looking for Mr. Turnbull."

"That's my name," replied the boss, and waited.

"My name is Standifer," began Jeff, smiling deprecatingly, "and I need a little help, Mr. Turnbull. I'm a deputy sheriff—trying to cut down this rustling—and yesterday we took six men to town. Bill Longyear and some of his gang. But I had to go away and leave a penful of weaner calves—"

"Who sent you to me?" demanded Turnbull. "Cap'n Bayless?"

"No—" and Jeff smiled again—"Ralph the Rover."

"Rover!" repeated the boss, rearing back.

"Yes, he said you didn't like him and probably had him in your black book—for a cow-thief or something like that. But I was asking for a special kind of man."

"What kind was that?" asked Turnbull gruffly.

"A man that was well known and respected by every body, and never told a lie in his life."

"Huh!" grunted the old man; but as he looked Jeff over, his lips curled in a grudging smile.

"What you want me to do?" he demanded.

"I want you for a witness," returned Standifer. "To send Bill Longyear to the Pen."

"And what about these calves?" inquired Turnbull.

"Well, there's lots of them—a couple of hundred, including the burned ones—and I want the weaners for evidence. Thought I'd round up some mother cows, down here on the plains, and see if they wouldn't own their calves."

"I can see," nodded the boss, "that you wasn't born yesterday. How do you know they ain't driven them away?"

"I don't," admitted Jeff. "That's why I'm in such a sweat. I rode out from town last night."

"And do you expect me," rumbled Turnbull, "to call off my cowboys to go out and gather those calves? But I'll do it, by Gad, if the whole round-up goes to hell. Things are getting pretty rank, and no mistake."

He strode off to the corral and as Jeff filled his plate again the cook favored him with a furtive wink.

"You're shore lucky, boy," he said. "Eat hearty."

Standifer ate, until Turnbull summoned him gruffly to the saddle and they headed for Rustlers' Canyon. The cowboys swung out below them, to rake the range for calfless cows, and by noon the bawling mothers drifted in. Some had been stabbed in the loin with a pocket-knife to keep them from calling their young, others had had their toes spread and a wedge jabbed through the membrane, making every step an agony. The cowboys removed the prods and drove them all in, and when they witnessed the scene in the weaning pen they called down a curse on all rustlers.

The motherless calves rushed about, running from cow to cow, bunting their flanks and demanded to be suckled; and fifteen calves in the course of one day were reunited with their mothers.

"It's a dodrammed shame!" muttered Turnbull, as they turned back with the sore-footed herd; and slowly, taking days to it, they drove them into Bitter-water, while the people rode out miles to see them. Never before had evidence so damning been gathered to prove the guilt of the rustlers, and even their best friends were alarmed. They still dominated the county and controlled its officials; but there was a packbox full of ears, picked up in the branding pen, which told a tale not easy to refute.

Here were the ears of Mill Iron cattle, cut to the swallow-fork and grub of Longyear's well-known ear-mark, and each key was proof not only of the owner but also of the man who had stolen it. But this boxful of severed ears, left so carelessly in the pen, revealed the earmarks not only of the Mill Irons but of men who had thought Longyear their friend. There were ears from his neighbors, the little men who had stood behind him when he had defied Captain Bayless to arrest him, and every ear represented a betrayal. There were Mormon ears, and Mexican ears, even ears from the mysterious Pig Pen, which was considered to be a straight, rustler brand. And there were murmurings when the ears were displayed.

Captain Bayless rode out to look over the herd and to tender congratulations to Standifer, but Jeff was grim and distant. Even when Annabelle came galloping up he did not talk with her long, for there were jealous eyes upon them. It was not as a Company man, not as the son-in-law of Bayless, that he wished to be known in this trial; but as an officer of the law who, without fear or favor, was engaged in stamping out theft. He was a deputy sheriff, not a hired detective, and there were men now who nodded when he passed.

Frank I. Turnbull rode with him to the jail-yard where a stout corral had been built for the weaners—and that in itself counted much. The FIT men, sometimes known as the "Fight Outfit", had been busily engaged for some years in a private war on all rustlers. And when old Frank quit his round-up to gather the stolen calves and qualify as a witness to their theft there were those who smelled smoke and sensed fire. The lone Ranger from Texas was no longer a friendless man, with no one but drunken Rover to stand by him. He had secured a powerful ally, a man who like himself hated rustling on general principles. Which was another reason why Jeff cut Bayless cold, for the Captain and Turnbull were enemies.

They had quarreled, in fact, over the one particular subject which had come between Standifer and his boss; but Turnbull had told Bayless to his face that he was harboring a gang of thieves. He had claimed, and brought evidence to prove it, that the Company's men were stealing his cows; and with his fighting men behind him he had patrolled the borders of his range and turned the Mill Iron cowboys back. Not for Jack Flagg, or his Wild Bunch, or the Captain himself, would he permit them to cross his line; and at last the big Company had been compelled to send representatives to the little FIT round-up. But that was better than war.

The weaner calves and their mothers, best evidence of all, were safely corralled that first night; and Captain Bayless offered the use of his town pasture to hold the rustlers' stolen herd. Special deputies were sworn in, to guard them under the protection of the court, and Smith Crowder himself took charge. But Old Frank merely grunted contemptuously, and in the morning every cow-brute was gone.

CHAPTER XXVI
Trial by Jury

THE QUARRELS BETWEEN Captain Bayless and Frank I. Turnbull, quarrels which at times had come close to war, were as nothing to the cursing and general vituperation which followed the loss of Longyear's calves. There was a hole in the fence on the opposite side of the pasture from where the sheriff's guards watched the gate, and the tracks of many shod horses led to the obvious conclusion that the cattle had been stolen for a purpose. But Turnbull went further, after trailing them for miles, and claimed that Jack Flagg had done it.

Captain Bayless brought forth proof, satisfactory to himself, that his range boss had been forty miles away. And Turnbull came back with the evidence of the horse-tracks to prove that Jack Flagg had been there. He knew Jack's tracks, and his horse's tracks, and the tracks of the Wild Bunch—and he professed to have discovered all three. But when the smoke had cleared away the fact still remained that the calves' value, as evidence, was gone.

No man could come into court and swear that any one of them had belonged to that stolen herd. They had been scattered in every direction and Jeff Standifer, for one, abandoned all hope of getting them back. On a range so swarming with rustlers that an honest brand was the exception there were hundreds of stolen calves. And in the strong corral beside the jail he still had the fifteen cows and the calves they had owned in the weaning pen. One cow and one calf was enough to convict and he slept out by the corral every night.

It was constructed of railroad ties and six strands of barbed wire, with a gate-lock that had only one key; and no man, day or night, was allowed to approach it except under the eyes of a guard. A great battle had begun, one which would determine for years whether the rustlers or the law was supreme; and as the long weeks dragged by with no relief from their misery the prisoners complained more and more bitterly.

They sent out word to their friends to come to their assistance, they engaged a lawyer to reduce their bail. But few if any friends responded and the Mormon judge was adamant. Their only relief lay in trial. Even if the Grand Jury indicted them the district judge who presided could grant them a reduction of bail; but for all their stealing there was not a man among them who could give sureties for five thousand dollars.

Jeff Standifer watched them narrowly as day after day they sweltered in the stinking jail. It was close and hot, and even at night the brick walls radiated heat. At first they had been defiant, secure in the thought that their friends would soon turn them loose; but after a month of restless waiting he saw them turn sullen and their lawyer was summoned again. What he did Jeff could only guess, but a week after the conference the district attorney acted.

In a letter citing the unrest which had been caused by the delay, and the emergency then existing, he requested a special session of the Grand Jury and an extra term of court. Then as the district judge returned and swore in the jury the gathering of the factions began. The spring round-up was over now and the hard-riding cattlemen had leisure to come to town. And every man, sooner or later, visited the corral in the jail-yard and gazed in at the weaner calves.

They were fat and plump now, watched over by hostile mothers who had not forgotten their ordeal, but their mangled ears and misbranded hips told the story of their theft all too plainly. Nor were they all Mill Irons—there were mother cows in the pen which belonged to neighbors and friends. The feeling ran high in the saloons and on the streets where cattle-owners and cowboys congregated; and Ralph the Rover, scouting around, brought the news back to Standifer that the rustlers were on the run.

They were divided among themselves, some standing up for Longyear and loudly denouncing the Company; and others who had suffered losses cursing the rustlers up and down and hoping they would get the limit. Then the Mill Iron boys rode in, abandoning their distant round-up, and in a day the sentiment changed. Jack Flagg was in the lead, covertly friendly to Bill Longyear though he did not visit the jail; but everywhere he went he rang money on the bar and invited friend and foe to drink.

It was like Court Day back in Texas, where many a border feud has been settled by an appeal to Judge Colt. Or the first trials by jury when ancient Norsemen, armed for war, lined up north and south before the Hill of Law, ready to fight at need for their friends. And here as in the days of Gunnar and Burnt Njal there were killers and trouble-makers in the throng.

From the steps of the jail, where he kept watch both over his prisoners and the evidence he had gathered to convict them, Standifer gazed across the track at the crowd of boisterous cowboys and wondered if they would get beyond bounds. The drinks were free every-where, for Jack Flagg and his gang had been setting them up all day. And on that day of days the Grand Jury would summon witnesses and consider the evidence of Bill Longyear's guilt.

In his office the district attorney had denied himself to all callers while he made out the writs of indictment, but Standifer had seen one man slip in and slip out again—Zeb Chambers, the attorney for the defense. More than he watched the seething street Jeff kept his eye on Sutton's office. What if the indictments were drawn up wrong? There was bad blood now between Standifer and Sutton, bad blood also between him and Smith Crowder; but Jeff's life itself might be the forfeit if Bill Longyear and his gang were released.

He lingered, irresolute, waiting impatiently for Rover to return from his tour of the saloons; but more and more it was borne in upon him that Sutton had gone over to the enemy. Was he going to throw the case? Over night the prisoners had assumed a sudden arrogance, making mention of a hereafter for smart detectives; and certainly, if they escaped the mesh of the law, he would have six more good reasons for leaving town. Captain Bayless in a pique would have nothing more to do with him, even Annabelle was distant and constrained; and Frank I. Turnbull, the one man he had counted on, had not come to court with his men. Only Rover remained to be his friend in need, and as he came hurrying Jeff went out to meet him.

"Hell in general," reported Rover. "They're out to git us, this time. Red the Killer is back in town."

"How do you know!" demanded Standifer. "Who told you!"

"A little bird—over in the Bird-cage," hinted Rover.

219

"And she says Flagg is just throwing money."

"Well, you give her this," said Jeff, handing over some bills. "It'll be no good to me if I'm dead. And tell her to spread the word that this town is too small for Red the Killer and me. I'll shoot it out with him on sight."

"All right," agreed Rover. "But, speaking of small towns, is it big enough to hold you and Jack?"

"It is," returned Standifer, "until I get through with these rustlers. But after they're gone, reducing the population by six, it'll be too small for Jack."

"I git you," nodded Rover. "One dog at a time. Have you heard the latest about Sutton? He was drinking with Flagg last night."

"I thought so!" burst out Standifer. "Here, watch these cows and calves—I'll be back."

Loosening his pistol in its holster he strode into the courthouse and straight up to Sutton's door.

"I want to see those indictments," he said, pushing in; and Sutton slammed the door shut.

His eyes were blazing with anger but one look at the Ranger convinced him it was no time for trifling. Without a word he handed them over and after one glance Standifer slapped them down on the table.

"They're no good!" he declared. "They won't hold!"

"How do you know?" demanded Sutton. "You haven't read them!"

"Now here!" began Jeff, pointing an accusing finger. "Do you want me to take this to the judge? You know how to draw up a legal indictment and, damn you, I want you to do it!"

He stepped back and waited and the district attorney met his eyes. Then he picked up the papers and tore them in half and Standifer strode out the door. His hunch had been right, after all.

Ralph the Rover was watching for him and when Jeff came back he pointed up the hall. The judge was beckoning Standifer into his chambers. What passed between them was secret and privileged, but when Jeff went out the judge gave him his hand.

"I am here," he said, "to support the law."

That was all, but the rustlers were indicted.

The swarming streets of Bitterwater were a riot that night when it became known that Bill Longyear must stand trial; and in the morning, when the drawing of the jury began, the courtroom was crowded to the doors. Smith Crowder fought his way through the jam in the corridors, summoning man after man for talesmen; and Sutton, deeply chastened, with the eyes of the judge upon him, challenged every rustler sympathizer that came up. If at any moment he had even distantly contemplated a dereliction of duty—and no one offered to accuse him—he had remembered his oath in time. His old confidence returned and as the representative of The People he bitterly arraigned the prisoners.

While the excitement was at its height Frank I. Turnbull rode into town at the head of twenty men. That was the beginning of the end and for the first time since his arrest Longyear lost his air of confidence. He lolled back easily as Standifer and Ralph the Rover gave their testimony and identified the calves, for they were both Company men. He knew and the jurors knew that they were in the pay of Captain Bayless—but Turnbull wore no man's collar. He was a man who stood alone and when he finished his testimony the rustlers knew they were doomed. Two days later the judge sentenced them to five years in the Penitentiary and Bitterwater went mad overnight.

CHAPTER XXVII
The Hold-Up

AFTER THE BIGGEST drunk in history—a drunk which strewed the streets of Bitterwater with men lying like dead and others spurred and battered in the fight—Captain Bayless fired Jack Flagg. He gave no reason, beyond the simple and sufficient one that he had come to town against orders, but the Mill Iron cowboys quit. They stood behind their chief to a man, and Bayless gave them their time. Then he wired back to Texas for gunmen and put the whole outfit afoot.

It had taken a continuous pecking, like water dropping on a stone, to wear away the Captain's resistance. In season and out of season he had stood up for his range boss and defended the integrity of his men. He had held out against all reason and the patent evidence of his own eyes, but the big drunk had been too much. The Mill Iron cowboys had spent a year's wages apiece and Bayless had not paid them a cent. From what other source could the money have come except from the sale of cattle, stolen from him while they drew his pay?

So the Captain gave them their time and put them afoot, that crowning humiliation of a cowboy; and while they besieged the O.K. Stable for mounts to return to the wagon Bayless guarded the horseherd, personally. The old six-shooters, which for years had been laid aside as unnecessary, were once more strapped on his hips; and more than one cowboy who owned a private mount lacked the nerve to face him and ask for it. He was mad—mad all over—and they had robbed him.

Jack Flagg stalked the street with the hangdog defiance of a man exposed at last in his treachery. The Captain had cursed him out and Flagg had had to take it, but now he was plotting revenge. From the saloons and back alleys he rounded up his men and bought them mounts with the limitless money he still flashed; and then under the eyes of the "Fight Outfit", who still guarded the jail, he rode out of town, an outlaw.

All through the wild night, while rumors of a rescue ran rife, Frank I. Turnbull and his warriors had camped outside the jail, drinking moderately, ready to turn back a rush. And now as they watched them leave they bristled back at their old enemies as if daring them to make a gun-play. It had been a long fight, with all the odds against them, but the FIT Outfit had won. Silent and brooding in his lonely cell the Rustler King awaited commitment to prison; and Jack Flagg, the Cowboy King, had left town.

The rustlers had left at daylight, those who could sit

a horse to ride, and Bitterwater was empty and still. The battle was over and the morning after had come— all that remained was to take Longyear to Yuma. But out on the range, carrying a rustler brand, ran thousands of cattle his gang had stolen. There were Hog Eyes and Frying Pans and the myriads of Pig Pens, all brands burned over the Mill Iron, and who would get them now?

This was the question over which the cowboys had fought on the streets of Bitterwater that night; and its answer, besides the bloody faces and broken heads, was the sudden hegira from town. The rustlers at dawn and Jack Flagg's men later had ridden away with a purpose; and Turnbull, for one, knew what it was. Two kings had been dethroned, six rustlers sent to prison and deprived of their hard-won spoils; but the cattle they had stolen still roamed the plains and the stealing would begin all over again. Perhaps they would even steal from him.

As the day wore on and others sought sleep Frank I. Turnbull began to pace the floor. All too well he could picture the drunken rage of the rustlers as they rode away to their homes. They were many and his men were few—and while he guarded the jail they could wreak a soul-satisfying revenge.

"Smith," he said at last as the heavy-eyed sheriff came out of his inner office, "I don't reckon you need me any more."

"I never did need you," answered Crowder gruffly. "What put that idee in your haid?"

"Your memory," retorted Turnbull, "is short as a

bear's tail. But I've got no time to argue. Come on, boys—we're going home."

The sheriff's eyes lit up balefully as his self-appointed guardians saddled their horses and hit the trail south. Within the last month so many men had come to help him that he had lost all but the semblance of authority. Jeff Standifer, Ralph the Rover, Frank Turnbull and his fighting men—but now the trial was over. Friends and enemies alike had gone charging out of town to tend to their immediate business, and the next day Crowder took over his.

"Mistuh Standifer," he began, when Jeff appeared along towards evening. "I won't be needing your services any more. This heah jail is a regular boars' den and I'm going to take those stinking prisoners and put them on the train for Yuma."

"But the law says," objected Standifer, "that a man can't be committed until five days after he's sentenced."

"Mistuh Standifer," replied the sheriff, "I know all about the law and I don't need any instructions from you, suh. You seem to have the idee that you're the boss around heah. But I'm the sheriff—you're only a deputy. And furthermore, dodram it, I'm getting good and tired of having you tell me my business."

The long period of strain had begun to tell on Crowder, after the old days when he had played pitch with his prisoners and lived at peace with mankind, and his voice broke to a peevish treble. He resented deeply the invasion of his rights by this detective brought from Texas; but most he resented the success of this last coup, when he had brought in six rustlers and convicted them. It was a reflection, in a way, on the efficiency of the sheriff, and another election was coming on.

Standifer eyed him shrewdly, suddenly mindful of Longyear's boast that he would never be taken to the Pen, but he answered with a smile.

"If you think," he said, "that I really enjoy it, hanging around your lousy old jail, you've got another think coming. But these men are my prisoners—I caught them and brought them in—and I'll see them to the door of the Pen."

"You will not!" returned Crowder stiffly. "Unless, of co'se," he sneered, "you go over my head again and appeal to the district judge. Because these six men have been committed into my custody, to be delivered at the Territorial Prison—nothing said about you, at all."

"Are you going to deliver them!" inquired Standifer. "Suppose the rustlers should stop the train—would you fight, or turn them loose?"

"Young man," quavered Crowder, "I've been sheriff for fo'hteen yeahs and never lost a prisoner on the train. And, being as Bill Longyear and his men have waived their legal rights, I'm going to take them— right now!"

"What—alone?" demanded Jeff, starting back; and Smith Crowder burst out cursing.

"Damn your heart!" he raged, "you git out of my sight, befoah I speak my whole mind. I don't need you and I don't want you. And furthermore, Mistuh Standifer, don't you make any moah cracks about *me*. I can tend to these prisoners, alone!"

He strode puffing into the cellroom to give his orders for the departure and Standifer crossed the track on the run. It was a day-and-night journey to the prison at Yuma and the rustlers would change cars twice. They had friends—and, more than friends, they had partners in crime who dared not let them talk. They would have to attempt a rescue, and Crowder was playing right into their hands.

From saloon to saloon Jeff went scouting for Rover, and when he found him he hustled him out.

"Get your rifle," he whispered, "and watch the train when it comes in. Smith Crowder is taking the prisoners to Yuma!"

"What—alone?" gasped Rover. "That old he-dog— he's sold out! He'll turn them boys loose, and I know it."

"Not while I'm on the job," returned Standifer. "I'm going to swing on and see this thing through. And say, Rover—tell Annabelle I'll be back!"

"Well, I should hope so!" grumbled Rover as he went for his gun. And when the train came rumbling in he had the prisoners nicely covered through the crack of a warehouse door.

They came out shackled together in pairs, with Smith Crowder limping pompously behind, and marched up the track to the smoker. He had a pistol on his hip, but he carried a heavy bag—and the trigger-finger of his right hand was gone. Bill Longyear looked back at him, then across at the saloons which so lately had swarmed with his friends. But the street was deserted and at a word from Crowder he led the way on to the train.

From the shelter of a coal-shed Jeff saw them filing in and swung up as the day-coach passed. He had tucked his two pistols under the slack of his shirt and pulled his hat down over his eyes, and as the train picked up speed he went ahead to the front platform and peered into the half-empty smoker. Smith Crowder—had seated his prisoners in the three farthest seats and was standing over them, talking. His fat face was working, his crab-like eyes bulged angrily; and when he ended the rustlers laughed. Standifer crouched low and watched them—was it possible that the sheriff had sold out to them openly and planned to bring all his work to naught?

Night was falling, the time was auspicious for a hold-up and the rescue of the prisoners; and still, his pistol within reach of Longyear's hand, the fat sheriff hovered over them, talking. His was more the good fellowship of a friend than the stern and watchful mien of an officer, and from the wealth of envenomed mirth that puffed out his red cheeks Jeff knew they were talking about him.

But did Crowder and the prisoners think they could ditch him that easy—merely by telling him to keep off the train? Did they imagine that, after working day and night to convict them, he would lie back and let them escape? Jeff clung tight to the swaying platform, watching every move they made, until suddenly a door slammed behind him.

In the dim light of a lantern Standifer was confronted by two trainmen who were looking him over suspiciously, and with a quick twist he flashed his star.

"I'm watching those prisoners!" he shouted to the conductor. "That's Bill Longyear and his gang, going to Yuma!"

"Well, why don't you go in there?" demanded the brakeman.

"I'm watching the sheriff, too," explained Jeff. "Figure on giving them a little surprise."

The conductor glanced into the smoker and beckoned Standifer back into the day-coach.

"Be careful, young man," he warned. "I don't want any shooting. The passengers might think it was a hold-up."

"That's just what's liable to happen," answered Jeff, "and I'll give you a little tip. If you see a bunch of cowboys flagging the train to stop, you signal the engineer to keep going. Anywhere within twenty miles now they're liable to spring it, so go through 'em like a bat out of hell."

The conductor grunted and went forward into the smoker where Standifer saw him talking with Crowder. Then with a hissing of air the brakes suddenly went on and the engineer whistled to stop. Jeff ran down the steps and saw a fire up ahead, a full shipping-pen and cattle-cars on the switch. Running figures came in view and a tall cowboy stood on the track, waving his hat for the train to stop. The brakes grabbed and as the train lost its impetus, Standifer leapt back and looked into the smoker. The conductor was just reaching for the signal-cord and when he pulled it the engineer whistled twice.

There was a lull, an easing of brakes, a slow picking up of speed and the cord was yanked again, insistently. Two shrill blasts made their answer, the engine labored with rapid puffs, and they glided into the light of the fire. From his hiding-place on the platform Jeff saw the men scatter, still frantically waving their hats; then with a thunder of wheels and steam the train rushed past them and the cowboys yelled a last, parting curse.

CHAPTER XXVIII
Confession

WITH A BROAD grin on his grimy face Standifer glanced back into the smoker, where Smith Crowder had drawn a gun on his prisoners, and the conductor beckoned him in. The sheriff was engaged in a violent altercation with Bill Longyear and the rest of his gang and Jeff sauntered in, unnoticed. But when, by chance, Crowder looked up and recognized him his troubled brow suddenly cleared.

"Good evening," nodded Standifer, glancing about, "I thought you might need a little assistance."

"Well, I do," admitted the sheriff. "These damned whelps are starting a riot, but here's one man that will never git away."

He fetched out a pair of handcuffs and snapped one

cuff over Longyear's wrist and the other to the iron seat.

"Break that, now," he said, "and I'll put the legirons on you. Come over heah!" And he shackled the rest to their seats.

"That's the trouble," he panted, "when you treat 'em like white folks. The next thing you know they start a break. I thought we were going to stop, back there."

"Nope," responded Standifer, "the conductor changed his mind. He's four hours late, already."

He glanced at the trainmen, who regarded him grimly, and Smith Crowder mopped his brow. In the confusion of the break he had not noticed the train speed up, passing the gang at the shipping-pen. All he knew was that his prisoners had suddenly got out of hand and started a small-sized riot.

"W'y, where did *you* come from?" he demanded of Jeff; and Standifer smiled understandingly.

"Just tagged along—I was going West, anyway. I Always wanted to see that prison down at Yuma."

"Well, heah's where you git your chance—with double mileage both ways," responded Crowder with a sigh. "Mind watching the prisoners a minute? I feel the need of a drink."

"No, I'll watch 'em all night," volunteered Standifer blithely; and sat down across the aisle.

Bill Longyear was excited. Every time the train slowed down he leaned over and peered out the window, glancing across at intervals at Jeff. But as they rumbled on across the plains and began the ascent of the high mountains he settled back with a curse. They had passed through the country of his rustler friends and no one had lifted a hand.

"You think you're smart, don't you?" he snarled as Standifer met his eyes; but Jeff only shrugged his shoulders.

"I was smart enough to ketch you, Bill," he said.

"You ain't half as smart as you think you are," railed Longyear. "I've been double-crossed by my friends. Say, what happened, back there where they flagged us?"

"Oh, nothing," answered the Ranger indifferently. "There was a big bunch of cowboys shipping cattle and a tall guy tried to stop us. Waved his hat, or something like that."

"Yes, and do you know who that tall guy was?"

"Well, he looked like Jack Flagg," stated Jeff.

"I'll bet ye it was Jack!" declared Longyear vindictively. "But he's so daggoned busy, running off my cattle, he doesn't give a damn for me! He promised me, blast his heart, I'd never see the Pen; but all the time he was figgering on ditching me. We were pardners with that Frying-Pan brand."

"I reckon that's what he was shipping, then," grinned Jeff. "I counted forty-four cars when we passed."

"Why the devil don't you go back and *git* him," complained Longyear, "instead of persecuting me this way? Ain't I had enough grief without you rubbing it in and follering me clean to the Pen?"

"You might get loose," suggested Standifer, "and come back and kill me, like you promised a time or two. I haven't forgotten, Bill, how you capped me into that dog-fight and hired Red the Killer to down me."

"I did not!" flared back Longyear. "That was all Jack Flagg's work, the dirty, double-crossing dog. I oughter knowed, right then, if he'd do a trick like that he'd ditch me, the first chance he got. And I've got a family, Jeff."

"Yes, I know," returned Jeff, "and you're going to a place where I certainly hate to send any man. They say that prison at Yuma is hell. But you boys were rustling, and you tried to kill me to boot, so I had to take you in."

"That's all right," sighed Longyear. "You treated us fair and square and I've got no big kick coming on that. But what about Jack Flagg and his Cowboys' Pool? Are you going to let them git away?"

"Never heard of a Cowboys' Pool!" responded Standifer bluffly; and the rustlers laughed him to scorn.

"Yes, you dodrammed Company man," taunted Tate Bascom, "you were mighty particular who you caught. There was Jack Flagg and the Wild Bunch and that whole Cowboys' Pool, hair-branding right under your nose, and by grab, you never even heard of it! You came clean out to Rustlers' Canyon and ran us poor suckers in—but umph-umm, never heard of the Pig Pens!"

"Oh, I've heard of the Pig Pens," answered Jeff, "but I never could find out who owned them. Of course I had my suspicions, on account of all that hair-branding—"

"Aw, you knowed!" laughed Bill Longyear, "but you're like Crowder and all the rest of them. You're standing in with the Pool."

"What—the sheriff?" exclaimed Standifer, glancing back at the rear seat where Smith Crowder was peacefully sleeping; and all the rustlers responded at once. Since they had lost in the game they took a malicious pleasure in pulling down those who had won.

"Of course!" they clamored in chorus.

"I never would've believed it," said Jeff. "I thought he was just chuckle-headed."

"Nope, he stood in with the gang," stated Longyear. "Been gitting his paws greased regular. You ought to heard what he said when he put us on the train—about what a danged fool you was."

"He told me that to my face," grinned Standifer. "But I kind of had a hunch something was wrong. Was he going to turn you boys loose?"

"Hell, no!" cursed Bascom. "It was that dirty dog. Jack Flagg. He was going to hold up the train and take us away from Smith. But what did the danged whelp do? He jest let the train go by, while he gathered all our cattle! But I'll git the scoundrel yet!"

"I doubt it," shrugged Jeff. "By the time you get back to Bitterwater Jack Flagg will be gone and forgotten."

"Well, I'll tell *you*, then," proposed Bascom, "and you go and git him. How's that, boys? Ain't that fair and square? What have we got to gain by holding out what we know? Let's tell 'im and let *him* grab Jack!"

"Yes, and maybe he can he'p us to git out of Yuma,"

suggested Longyear with a crafty smile. "How about it, Jeff? Is it a go?"

Standifer glanced about the car where all the other occupants were sprawling in uneasy sleep, and his eyes came to rest on Smith Crowder. Big and gross, with fat jowls and shaking paunch, he was only the husk of a sheriff; but still he was Jeff's chief.

"Listen, Bill," he replied. "I'm a deputy sheriff, with orders to take you to Yuma, and all hell won't keep me from doing it. I play straight, myself, no matter who's crooked, so I guess we can't make a trade."

"Yes, but look what we've got," argued Longyear.

"Jest think of all we can tell you. I'll give you the names of every man in the Cowboys' Pool and I'll tell you where they keep their stuff. They've double-crossed me— why shouldn't I double-cross them? Don't you want to git Jack Flagg?"

"I don't need any help to get Flagg," responded Standifer; and instinctively he touched his gun.

"Do you aim to kill him?" demanded Bascom eagerly. "Then listen—I'll tell you something. They're raking the range right now for their Pig Pen stuff; and when it's all gathered they're going! The whole gang—up to Northern Colorado—but you can ketch him if you start back now. If you don't, Jack Flagg will be gone!"

"Let 'im go," shrugged Jeff. "I'll find him."

"You'll find hell," jeered Longyear. "Shall we tell him about it, boys? Jack has hired a man to kill you."

"I know that, too," nodded Standifer.

"Well, listen," insisted the rustler. "Here's something you don't know—the men in that Cowboys' Pool! Git a paper and we'll give you their names."

"Now you're talking," said Jeff, "and I'll tell you what I'll do. You give me the name of every Jack Flagg man and I'll speak a good word to the judge. That's all, boys, but it will help and—"

"Git your paper!" they shouted in a chorus; and Jeff wrote long and fast in his book. He could hardly believe that storekeepers and railroad men, lawyers and bankers, were all in the ring, hardly write down the names as they came—and when, as the train pulled into a station, Smith Crowder came down the aisle, Jeff did not even look up.

The sheriff was heavy-eyed from his broken sleep but as he heard what the rustlers were saying he stopped short and listened, aghast. They were confessing to Standifer—and all the calves they had stolen were still running free on the range. With ponderous stealth Crowder tiptoed down the aisle and snatched up a telegraph blank. He wrote feverishly, looking up as he signed his name, but Jeff was still leaning over his book. Crowder dropped off and filed his telegram, and when Standifer glanced up to greet him he responded with a Judas-like smile.

CHAPTER XXIX
The Cowboys' Pool

WITH A FULL CONFESSION from the rustlers in his inside pocket Jeff was afire to rush back to Bitterwater. At last he had broken the front of the organized gang which had resisted him at every turn. He had penetrated the charmed circle and learned the secrets of the Pool, whose very name had been hidden until now. He had the goods on Jack Flagg and many a smug business man, but he dared not leave the prisoners.

Smith Crowder was bland and placating, praising Standifer for his acumen, placing the rustlers entirely in his charge; but all the time Jeff knew that his enemies had been warned, that the clean-up even then was going on. When he landed in Bitterwater hired gunmen would be waiting for him, to stop him before he could talk. Jack Flagg might even be gone. But Standifer had worked too long to lose his prisoners now and he guarded them to the prison gates. But when the steel doors clashed behind them he turned back on the run and caught a fast train, eastward bound.

Another night and day dragged by as he sweltered in the desert heat, and then they toiled up over the mountains and thundered down towards the Little Colorado. When the snow was on the ground he had rolled into Bitterwater and seen the station crowded with rustlers.

They had come down to kill him or run him out of town, but Annabelle had saved the day. With true Western chivalry they had made way for the bride—all except Flagg, and he had taken the count. But would the rustlers make way again? Jeff loosened his guns in their holsters as the engine whistled to stop and set himself grimly for the fray.

How easy it would be to go back to the sleeper and ride the train through to Texas! He was worn out with the fighting, dead on his feet from loss of sleep; and after all who would care? Only Annabelle and Rover, that stout-hearted friend who had never failed him yet. But the honor of the Rangers was at stake and Jeff swung down and stared out into the night.

The broad platform, which he had expected to find crowded with rustlers, was empty except for one man. He lurked furtively in the shadows, gliding warily towards him, and Standifer came to a crouch.

"Who's that?" he challenged sharply; and from the darkness there came a low laugh.

"W'y, hello, Good Eye!" hailed a mocking voice. "Still hiding behind a blade of grass?"

It was Ralph the Rover, hurrying towards him.

"Where's the gang?" demanded Standifer, his hand still on his gun; and Rover laughed again.

"Done gone!" he pronounced. "Tuk to their holes like prairie-dogs. The day after you left the word came back that Bill Longyear and his rustlers had confessed, and that night the whole passel skipped out. Yes, indeedy—some of our most prominent citizens!"

"They'd better skip," said Jeff. "I've got the dead

wood on all of them. Don't look for Smith Crowder to come back. But say, Rover, where's Jack Flagg?"

"Oh, he's around," answered Rover. "Cap'n Bayless jest heard that he and his gang were shipping cattle, up the track."

"Pulling out," nodded Standifer. "They'll put up a fight if they're monkeyed with."

"That's jest it," observed Rover enigmatically. "The Cap'n was kinder waiting on you. He's got four Texas gunmen already, but seems like they're bashful with strangers."

"Oh, hell!" sighed Jeff. "What I need is a little sleep. But plenty chance to rest after we're dead."

Now that his enemies had fled a great weariness had come over him, but he saddled King Cole and rode forth. Captain Bayless was waiting in the Company corral with four silent men behind him and they took the narrow road up the track. Nothing was said but Jeff was given the lead, and far ahead they saw a glow against the clouds. A train glided towards them down the grade, and against the glare of its headlight Standifer glimpsed a string of cattle cars, lined up before a shipping-pen.

"That's them!" pronounced Rover, spurring eagerly forward; and they went up the track at a lope. From the cover of the darkness they could see the forms of men as they punched the cattle up the chute, and as they halted to reconnoiter they heard the *puff, puff* of an engine, kicking another car down to be loaded. It was all very methodical and business-like, but Bayless cursed under his breath.

"Jeff," he said, riding closer, "I've been the biggest fool in the world. It makes my blood boil to think of Jack Flagg deliberately shipping out my stock. I'm sorry I ever opposed you—it has cost me thousands of dollars!"

"Sure has," agreed Standifer. "And if we ride in on them now it's likely to cost you your life. That's Jack Flagg and his Cowboys' Pool, shipping out their Pig Pen stuff, and I reckon they'll be on the prod."

"Oh, don't think of me!" protested the Captain. "All I ask is a chance to shoot it out with the scoundrels before they escape with my cattle. And hurry, Jeff— they may go any time."

"All right," agreed the Ranger. "But we'd better ride around them, so we can flag that engineer if he starts. There's some crooked work going on and I wouldn't put it past them to pull out, the first shot that's fired. The cattle inspector and the train crew are in on it some way, and we don't want to lose those calves."

He swung out into the sagebrush and led the way around the shipping-pen, where by the light of two fires men were working in frantic haste, punching the cattle up into the cars. Who they were no one could tell but that they would fight was a certainty, for thousands of dollars were at stake. A cloud of dust over the corrals showed the presence of still more cows and by the light of dodging flares they could see big-hatted cowboys, swarming up over the top of the chute. Only the glare from the firebox and the *chuh, chuh* as it spotted the cars revealed the existence of the engine—the headlight had been turned off—but as

240

Jeff and his Rangers crossed the track ahead of it a heavy freight came toiling up the grade. Almost before they knew it the powerful headlight had reached them, silhouetting the dim figures by the pen; and not a hundred yards before them, standing upright on the track, Standifer saw a man with a gun.

He was a rustler scout, posted to protect them from surprise, and as the Rangers wheeled out into the sagebrush he emptied his six-shooter and yelled.

"Come on!" shouted Jeff, spurring forward. But as they galloped towards the pens the standing engine opened its eye like some monster of the night. In an instant every rider stood out as plain as day, but Captain Bayless was not to be denied.

"Follow me, boys!" he cried, taking command by instinct; and, swinging out into the darkness of the plains, he charged in on the pens. Alarmed by their approach, though they could no longer be seen, the rustlers opened fire at random; but the Rangers did not reply. On his thoroughbred racer the Captain led the way, eager to close in and shoot it out. Jeff and Rover followed close behind. But before they had come within pistol-shot the freight train thundered past the pen.

On the tops of cars and chutes, where they had mounted up to look, the huddled rustlers suddenly found themselves exposed to the merciless glare of its headlight. Every man stood out plainly and, looming above the rest, Captain Bayless beheld Jack Flagg, himself.

"Give 'em hell, boys!" he shouted, taking a shot

from the darkness; and at the first volley the startled rustlers stampeded. Then the freight engine which had exposed them moved as suddenly past and left them in Stygian darkness. Only the clanking of wheels told of the long train that followed it, but as the Rangers charged in blindly Jeff Standifer, looking back, saw another light stab the void. The switch-engine had come to life—and that clanking was of cattle-cars, moving slowly up to take the main track.

Around the shipping pens there was a melee of fleeing horsemen shooting wildly, and the yell of pursuing men; but as the jerk of the switch-engine yanked the cattle-train from end to end, Jeff reined in King Cole and turned back. Through the sagebrush and along the track on the cleared right-of-way they went at a smashing gallop, slipping and stumbling in dark holes but gaining on the spot ahead, where the headlight turned night into day.

The train hammered across the switch and headed up Puerco Pass, swaying and shackling as it picked up speed; but lion-hearted King Cole did not slacken his stride, though his breath came in great, choking gasps. And Jeff in the saddle gave him his head and rode light until suddenly the engine was beside them. There was a glare from the firebox as the door was flung open, a roar and the hiss of steam, and Standifer leaned over and swung up into the cab.

"Slow down!" he ordered, whipping out his gun; and the engineer threw on the air. In his last desperate coup Jack Flagg had lost again and nothing was left but revenge.

CHAPTER XXX
The Street of Death

ON HIS COT IN THE deserted jail whose last tenant had departed Standifer slept until the sun rose, burning hot. It was all over now, this battle which had lasted so long. Bill Longyear was in Yuma, Jack Flagg and his gang had fled, the Cowboys' Pool had been wrecked overnight. There was peace now—time for dozing, watching the sun rays mount higher; time for bathing, a clean shave, fresh clothes. He was stamping on his best boots for a visit to Annabelle when Rover appeared in the doorway.

"Say!" he said, stepping in mysteriously. "Have you heard that Red is in town?"

"Nope," answered Standifer, "but you're liable to hear anything. I'm on my way to see Annabelle."

"Well, you'd better put on a coat of mail," advised Rover. "The rustlers are out to git you, for revenge."

"That's all right," grinned Jeff. "We licked 'em last night and I reckon we can do it again. What did the Captain have to say about those calves?"

"He was so mad—and so glad—he ain't quit cussing yet. But say, Jeff—Flagg's in town!"

Standifer stopped in the middle of brushing his hair and laid the comb down carefully.

"Who told you?" he asked at last.

"Well, that little bird that lives over at the Birdcage. Mamie Sloper, the gal he made Queen."

"I—see," nodded Jeff. "She's got it in for him now."

"Yes, she wants to git him killed," admitted Rover.

"Umm," murmured Standifer, surveying his pardner thoughtfully. "Do you reckon he'll stand up and fight?"

"Not him!" declared Rover. "He's got a yaller streak lately. That's why he brought back Red."

"Well, in that case," said Jeff. "I'll have to call you in, Rover. Are you game to shoot it out?"

"I'll take 'em both on!" offered Rover valiantly. "Because you've got Annabelle, Jeff."

"Much obliged," grunted Standifer. "But that ain't necessary. I can kill my own snakes, yet."

"Yes, but these dirty whelps will be laying for you," objected Rover. "Trying to pot you from some side alley. I'll jest take my rifle and scout around through town. And believe me, I'll smoke 'em out."

"You take care of Red," Jeff suggested gently. And he belted on his second gun.

"Where you going?" demanded Rover. "Across the track to see Annabelle? She sent word not to come!"

"Not to come!" echoed Standifer. "Why not?"

"Well—I reckon she's heard that Jack is in town!"

And Rover nodded wisely.

"Listen, Rover," spoke up Jeff. "You know as well as I do that I've got to shoot it out with Flagg. And at the same time I want to see Annabelle. Do you think I'm going to hide because that whelp is in town? Go on over and bring me my horse."

"Sure," agreed Rover. "Anything to oblige. And don't you be afraid of Red. I'm going to hide in the freight shed with my Forty-five Seventy and the first move he makes I'll down him."

"You do it," said Standifer, "and you can have my shirt, Rover. The best pardner a man ever had!"

He held out his hand and Rover gripped it hard, then sloped across the track for King Cole.

Standifer took out his pistols and spun the cylinders thoughtfully, testing their action while he waited for his horse. It was just what he had expected but, coming as it did, he muttered at his fate. Ever since he had struck the country Jack Flagg had been his enemy—but he had lost, and he would lose again. But what could Jeff say to Annabelle? And how like a woman it was to bring on the quarrel and then try to stave off its end!

He paced the floor restlessly, peering out from the darkened window at the drab line of stores that made the town. They were all in one row on the south side of the railroad, facing the wide road that extended along the track; and between every house there was some space or alley where a lurking assassin could hide. But Ralph the Rover from the freight shed could command them all with his rifle—and when had Rover ever failed?

Standifer stepped up on King Cole and crossed the track slowly, watching each doorway and alley as he passed; but as he reined in before the hotel and waved his hand to Annabelle she beckoned him frantically inside.

"Why, Jeff!" she cried as she ran out to meet him, "didn't Rover deliver my message? I sent word not to come!"

"Well, I don't blame you," he smiled. "But being as I'm here—"

"Come in!" she said, dragging him through the door.

He glanced up and down the street, which was suspiciously empty, and across at Rover's freight-shed. Then he submitted, for Annabelle was in earnest.

"Don't you know," she demanded, "that Jack Flagg is in town? He's come here on purpose to kill you!"

"Think so?" he inquired. "I don't believe he's got the nerve. But who was telling you, Annabelle?"

"Come in here!" she commanded, whisking him into the best parlor and shutting the door with a slam. And as she turned she eyed him reproachfully.

"Jeff Standifer," she began, "I don't believe you love me! You never do a thing I ask you!"

"Oh, I don't know," he replied. "Didn't I marry you, Annabelle? Although I haven't made much of a husband!"

"Now you quit your teasing!" she scolded. "Didn't I tell you not to come? Think how I'd feel if Jack should kill you!"

"Yes, and think how *I'd* feel," he countered. "But don't you worry about Jack. God Almighty hates a coward, and any man that will hide hasn't got the nerve to shoot."

"But Red's here, too!" she quavered. "I just know something will happen. Why couldn't you wait a while?"

"Well, I've waited a long time," he said. "How about it—don't I get a kiss?"

"Do you want one?" she asked, looking up; and

suddenly her voice was soft.

"Yes, I do," he answered huskily. "I think a lot of you, Annabelle."

"Then I'll give you one!" she burst out impulsively, throwing her arms around his neck. "Oh, Jeff!" And she held him close.

It was a new experience for Standifer and his hands trembled as he put hers aside.

"Do you love me?" she demanded as she looked up into his eyes. "Sometimes I have a feeling that you never take me seriously—that you treat me just like a child. And then when you come back, without even writing me a letter, and speak to me the way you did then, I forget all about being mad. You do love me—don't you, Jeff?"

She laid hold of him insistently, drawing his lips down closer, but Jeff held his head up erect. There was a purpose behind her caresses—she was trying to break his courage, to wean him away from the fight. But he had sensed her subterfuge in time.

"I'll tell you later," he jested. "After we find out for sure whether you don't stack up a widow. Turn me loose, now—I've got to go."

"Go where?" she demanded breathlessly. "You aren't going up the street?"

"I sure am," he said. "And all the Jack Flaggs this side of hell can't turn me back from it, either."

"But he'll kill you, Jeff—I know it!"

"That's a fine, cheerful way for a wife to talk!" he chided. "Do you want to break my nerve? Now you just give me one more kiss and tell me to come back to you and—" He smiled as she leapt into his arms.

"Yes, yes—do come back!" she whispered. "Don't let him kill you, Jeff. Be careful—he's so treacherous. And look behind you, Jeff. Good-bye!" And she kissed him again.

"Good-bye, Pet," he said and, putting her absently aside, he stepped out on the street.

Across the track at the freight-shed he saw Ralph the Rover, crouching down behind some bales. A man or two was on the street. But at sight of Jeff they stepped into the first doorway and he swung up on his horse. With King Cole between his knees he could charge.

The sun had never seemed so bright, the world so fair as now when the end might be near. A new strength had come over him and he gazed about calmly as he rode up the Street of Death. Somewhere behind those false fronts and broken-down gates his enemies lay listening for his step. But they feared him, they hid, and if God hated a coward His curse lay upon them now. He rode on and no one stepped out.

Up the street, sitting sidewise to watch each alley and door, he rode proudly, challenging his foes; and Annabelle who had fled upstairs to the gallery gazed after him, hardly breathing. She had choked back the vain beseechings which had risen to her lips. Should she break his nerve when he was going out to fight? And she knew he would never relent. Not since that fateful day when he had stepped off the train and defended her against Jack's drunken kisses had he given up the will to fight. But her heart almost stopped as she watched.

As tranquil as a cowboy returning to the wagon after a day in the frontier town, unafraid of their bullets he rode the length of the street, and no one rose to shoot. But as he passed the Company House and straightened up in the saddle Jack Flagg stepped out on the Headquarters gallery and Annabelle uttered a scream. For his hand had shot out and she caught the gleam of a gun, pointed full at Standifer's back. She screamed again as the heavy pistol went off and Jeff ducked down behind his horse. But when she opened her eyes he had whirled King Cole and was charging back, straight at his foe.

On the porch above, Flagg fired again and again, working faster as Standifer approached; and in Jeff's hand, like a torch, his own pistol smoked, yet neither one went down. They came face to face, leaning forward and shooting desperately; and then Flagg dropped his gun. He slumped back suddenly and down the long steps Annabelle saw him come tumbling to the ground. It was over, and Rover gave a shout.

But as Standifer reined in beside his fallen enemy, swiftly loading his empty pistol, Annabelle saw Red the Killer run out of a doorway and look up and down the street. For a moment he hesitated, then his rifle came up and he drew a bead on Jeff. Her heart stopped, she closed her eyes, but when she opened them at the shot it was Red who lay on the ground. Ralph the Rover had shot him first, and Jeff still sat his horse.

Annabelle found herself running up the street, oblivious of everything but him; and when he saw her he stepped down quickly. Rover was standing beside him, blowing the smoke from his rifle barrel, there was a huddle of men around Flagg; but the eyes that met hers were strange. Jeff was calm but a new light had come into his eyes that made them gleam like steel.

"I'm all right," he said gently as she leapt into his arms and gave him an unnoticed kiss. "Go back to the hotel, Annabelle."

"Why—why, Jeff!" she cried, staring back at him. But the look in his eyes did not change and she turned away from him, weeping.

CHAPTER XXXI
The Bull-Fiddle

ANOTHER SANDSTORM had come up and the littered street of Bitterwater was obscured by a curtain of dust. Yet from her lookout on the gallery of the hotel Annabelle had seen the grim work go on. A coroner's jury had viewed the bodies, Jeff and Rover had come and gone; and then for two days in an agony of waiting she had watched the street in vain.

They were riding, fighting the wind in a vengeful quest for rustlers, oblivious of her and how she suffered; and yet if he would only come back she felt that she could still forgive Jeff. It was his way and nothing would change him—he was a warrior, like the proud men of old. But two days, without a word or a look—

and that terrible light in his eyes!

The sandstorm had gone down when she saw him riding in and she ran out to meet him joyously.

"Oh, Jeff!" she cried, "I'm so glad to see you!" And he glanced over at Rover with a grin.

"Good-bye!" responded Rover promptly; and he clanked into the Bucket of Blood.

"I'm awful dirty," began Standifer, wiping the dust from his eyes; but she dragged him in through the door.

"I don't care!" she laughed recklessly and, safe in the best parlor, she welcomed him with a kiss. "I'm so glad," she murmured, and sighed. But Standifer regarded her curiously.

"This is more than I'd expected," he said, "after the killing, and all the rest. But—I'm glad you can understand, Annabelle. This is a hard country and a rough life, but I reckon it's over with. Every rustler in the country has skipped."

"And are you going to quit?" she asked.

"There's only one way to do that," he grinned, "and that is to get out of town. Your old man is a regular slave-driver."

"What? Did he send you out there?" she flared up. "Without even letting you say good-bye? Oh, Jeff! And I thought you didn't care!"

"Well, sit down," he said ponderously, "and let's talk it over. I'm kind of tired, myself."

He settled back in the plush davenport which was Mother Collingwood's pride and met her eager eyes gravely.

"This joke of ours," he began, "about being married and all that, didn't turn out quite the way we expected. But it's over, and that's enough. Jack Flagg is dead and there's no one to bother you, so I reckon my work is done."

"Are you going—home?" she faltered; and reached out and clutched his hand.

"That depends," and he smiled, "on how you look at it, Annabelle. Now that the war is over I'm free to admit I didn't expect to come out alive. So that explains, if it needs any explaining, why I was game to get married, or anything. And when this last trouble came up I thought I'd go out fighting, if only to do honor to the widow!"

He took her hand in his and Annabelle eyed him earnestly.

"Well, of course," she said, "I wouldn't be a widow, but I'd feel just as bad as a real one. It seems as if we've been married for years. We've quarreled, and kissed and made up again, for all the world like married folks."

"Yes, we have," he admitted, "and I'll tell you something, Annabelle. I didn't think it was necessary to mention it before, since I was liable to get bumped off anyway; but ever since we stepped off that train together we've been legally man and wife."

"Why, Jeff!" she cried starting back. "Why, what do you mean?" she asked.

"Well," he said, "of course I had no intention of holding you to the bargain. It was all done on the spur of the moment in order to protect you from Flagg. But when a man publicly acknowledges a woman as his wife, and contributes to her support, the common law makes them man and wife."

"And were we really married, all the time?" she gasped. "Why didn't you tell me, Jeff?"

"You had enough to worry about," he smiled, "without having that on your mind. And I thought, if anything should happen to me, it might be better if you didn't know."

"Why, Jeff!" she exclaimed. "And I thought you were so brutal, when we quarreled about my dancing with Jack. But are we really married, now?"

She gazed up at him breathlessly and Standifer took her hand.

"That's for you to say, Annabelle," he said at last. "I've never felt so married in my life, not even when you used to scold me, but—"

"Then we're married!" she cried, throwing her arms around his neck and giving him a joyous kiss. "But to think of you, living in that dirty old jail—and just to make it easy for me. Only—what will people say?"

"Never mind," grinned Jeff. "Let 'em talk all they want to. It will help them forget their troubles. But say, how would you like to catch the train for California and get married again, in style?"

"Why, you darling!" she beamed, springing up to hug him rapturously. "But how much time have we got?"

"About an hour," he said. "Number Nine is late again."

"Oh, Number Nine!" she exclaimed. "That's the

same train we came in on. But don't tell a single soul! Don't even come back for me—we'll pretend to meet by accident and then we won't have to explain!"

"All right," he agreed. "If that ain't somebody at the keyhole. I thought I saw an ear there, just now."

"Why no!" she responded after a leap to the door; and when he laughed she kissed him again. Then she flew up the stairs to begin her packing and Jeff went out, walking on air.

The sandstorm had gone down, leaving a yellow glow in the west where the sun was sinking low, when Number Nine whistled to stop. Annabelle ran to the station, Jeff joined her dressed in his best, and then the engine stopped up the track. It was taking water at the tank.

"Do you remember," she asked, "how the train stopped before? And we looked out and saw the crowd? And then, just as it started, 'I heard that awful bull-fiddle—and I didn't have a husband anywhere!"

She giggled and clutched his arm like the Annabelle of old; but as they stood waiting on the platform there was a jangle from across the street and the *boom, boom* of a big, bass drum. Then from the Bucket of Blood, Ralph the Rover came running with a huge box under his arm.

"Oh, horrors!" exclaimed Annabelle; and the next moment the bull-fiddle let out its raucous alarm. Someone emptied a six-shooter, trumpets and cow-horns joined in, and the *charivari* charged down upon them. In the lead came Rover, hugging the bull-fiddle as he ran, and as the engine whistled twice and rum-

254

bled down towards the station he set it down and grabbed the rawhide bow. Annabelle screamed and closed her ears as the great box gave out a roar; but she was laughing, with tears in her eyes.

The train ground to a stop and the porter dropped off—the same porter who had tended them before—and suddenly the turmoil ceased.

"I thank you, boys," cried Annabelle, "for your kind attentions, and I hope you'll all wish us happiness. Good-bye!" And she waved her hand.

"Good-bye, Rover," called Standifer, rushing back to shake hands with him; and Annabelle followed close behind.

"Good-bye!" she smiled; and before he knew it she had kissed Ralph the Rover on the cheek.

He stood up, bowing bravely, waving his hat as they rolled away and Annabelle brushed away a tear.

"Poor Rover!" she murmured, and sighed.

"The best damned pardner a man ever had," said Jeff. And Rover waved again.

Center Point Publishing
600 Brooks Road ● PO Box 1
Thorndike ME 04986-0001 USA

(207) 568-3717

US & Canada:
1 800 929-9108